CO-AUZ-599

Praise for the Previous Writings of Charles Neider

"Very interesting and artistically remarkable. Written with a fine sensibility. . . . An excellent piece of narration."—**Thomas Mann**

"Instead of 'characters,' Neider gives us recognizable Americans. That's what makes the stunning difference."—**Saul Bellow**

"Very interesting, chiefly perhaps because of its human tensions." —**E. M. Forster**

"Achieved writing and rare content."—**Marianne Moore**

"Remarkable for its extreme truthfulness. I wish I possessed the author's penetrating acuteness of vision."—**Aldous Huxley**

"A gem of literary art. . . . I don't know whether to admire more the skill with which the author manages the subtly complex story or the beauty of the language in which he tells it."—**Max Eastman**

"Beautifully written . . . compelling, exotic, almost mysterious." —**Mark Schorer**

"[Neider's book] provides a vivid and compelling picture. . . . It is nothing short of a public service to the human race. . . . Extraordinarily well-written."—**Norman Cousins**

"I am really grateful to Charles Neider for his new book, with its human freshness and its exaltation."—**Alfred Kazin**

"Absorbingly readable, informative, with moments of high suspense." —**Edmund Fuller**

The

GROTTO BERG

The
GROTTO BERG

Two Novellas

CHARLES NEIDER

INTRODUCTION BY CLIVE SINCLAIR

Cooper Square Press

First Cooper Square edition 2001

This hardcover edition of *The Grotto Berg: Two Novellas* is an original publication. It is published by arrangement with the author.

The Grotto Berg: Two Novellas copyright © 1997, 2001 by Charles Neider
Introduction copyright © 2001 by Clive Sinclair

Published by Cooper Square Press
An Imprint of the Rowman & Littlefield Publishing Group
150 Fifth Avenue, Suite 911
New York, New York 10011

Distributed by National Book Network

Library of Congress Cataloging-in-Publication Data

Neider, Charles, 1915-
      The Grotto Berg : two novellas / Charles Neider.
         p. cm.
      Contents: The Grotto Berg—The left eye cries first.
      ISBN 0-8154-1123-5 (cloth : alk. paper)
      I. Title.

   PS3564.E268 G76 2000
   813'.54—dc21
                                          00-064389

♾™ The paper used in this publication meets the minimum requirements of American National Standard for Information Sciences—Permanence of Paper for Printed Library Materials, ANSI/NISO Z39.48-1992.
Manufactured in the United States of America.

CONTENTS

Introduction by Clive Sinclair
ix

The Grotto Berg
1

The Left Eye Cries First
83

INTRODUCTION

Clive Sinclair

An iceberg, it is common knowledge, conceals the bulk of its mass below the surface. All that is visible is the glittering tip. Charles Neider's "Grotto Berg" is no exception. Before you encounter its exhilarating charms, permit me to lead you on a tour of its hidden depths, and thereby reveal a few things about its extraordinary author you might not otherwise have known.

When England's Princess Elizabeth was crowned Queen Elizabeth II in 1953, my school held a costume party. I went dressed as a cowboy, with ersatz Stetson, neckerchief, fancy vest, and little six-gun in a plastic holster. I was five. My role model was Roy Rogers. On Sunday afternoons I would watch him prance across the television screen on his golden steed (now stuffed, like the couch on which I sat). Authentic it was not.

If only I had known Charles Neider back then. He too lived on a ranch (albeit temporarily) and rode through the canyons of California on a palomino, but there the similarities with Roy Rogers ended. Neider traveled on horseback and later made himself familiar with frontier hardware, because he was determined that his peerless novel of the Old West, *The Authentic Death of Hendry Jones,* would indeed be as authentic as he could make it. Consequently he wore a Colt .45 on his hip for two straight months, the traditional rig strapped to his right thigh except when he slept. He even practiced the draw for hours in front of a large mirror, until his fingers bled.

After publication the movie rights to the novel (his second) were acquired by Marlon Brando, who retitled the subsequent film *One-Eyed Jacks.* Neider was not encouraged to visit the set, probably because of the vast distance between the shooting-script and its source. One day, however, Brando's father invited the banished author to see some rushes. Brando, Neider noted, had stuck his pistol in the wide cummerbund that encircled his waist. Brando Sr. asked his opinion. "First time he'd draw that gun he'd blow his balls off," observed Neider. "Talk to him about it," urged Brando Sr. "He admires you. You're the only one he'll listen to." Others tried to pick his expert brain, among them the original screenwriter, Sam Peckinpah no less, who habitually called Neider "Master." A genuine man of the West, you'd conclude.

Wrongly. Charles Neider is a Method writer, just as Marlon Brando is a Method actor.

As a matter of fact, he was born in Odessa, Ukraine, like that other tough Jew-on-a-Horse, Isaac Babel. They were fellow citizens for a mere five years. In 1920 Neider's family left for America while Babel elected to ride with the Cossacks, an experience that inspired his famous book of stories, *Red Cavalry.* Speculating as to why a bespectacled Jew should be so attracted to anti-Semitic centaurs, the critic Lionel Trilling cited an episode in Babel's boyhood, one that caused him to redefine his notions of paternal omnipotence. The young writer-to-be had the misfortune to witness his father, helpless on his knees, petitioning a mounted Cossack. The Cossack responded politely enough, saying, "At your service," while completely ignoring the salient fact that a mob was looting the family store. "The sons of such men have much to prove, much to test themselves for," concluded Trilling, "and, if they are Jewish, their Jewishness is ineluctably involved in the test."

In *The Authentic Death of Hendry Jones* Neider also writes about violent souls, about the brotherhood of badmen; he in effect reworks (and relocates) the mythic confrontation of Pat Garrett and Billy the Kid. Trying to find an explanation for his own interest in mayhem, he notes that his new life began in Richmond, Virginia, and that he was wont to camp beside Civil War trenches in the vicinity. In those days, he recalls, it was still possible to root around and find rusted pots and musket balls. These were more than inanimate artifacts; a visit to the Confederate Museum in Richmond, with its photographs and displays of bloodstained uniforms, brought them vividly to life—*Red Cavalry* meets *The Red Badge of Courage,* as it were.

However, it might be more pertinent, following Trilling's lead, to consider a direct encounter with belligerence in the Old Country, which certainly made a deep impression upon Neider's receptive psyche (remember he was not yet six when he emigrated). Although a native of Odessa, he actually spent the formative years of his childhood in the neighboring town of Akkerman (Turkish for White City), on the western bank of the Dniester. When World War I broke out, the Axis powers immediately exploited its vulnerability. "I experienced the shelling of Akkerman as the Rumanians prepared to occupy it," recalls Neider. "One of my childhood memories is of crouching with my Jewish parents, who were very aware of pogroms, in our cellar during bombardment. It wasn't a pleasant experience to see adults, on whom I was totally dependent, in a state of fear and sometimes terror." Now it so happens that the Pat Garrett stand-in, the sheriff who shoots Hendry Jones (a.k.a. the Kid), is called Dad Longworth. "I used the word instinctively," claims Neider in an unpublished postscript, a reflex prompted, perhaps, by that ancient memory. Enough! It is not my purpose to psychoanalyze Neider. Besides it would be an error to overemphasize the violence in his work (or in Babel's, for that matter); more important to both is camaraderie, the dynamics of men working together in difficult circumstances, a theme taken to the extreme in "The Grotto Berg."

There are many other indicators of a shared sensibility; for example, both are extremely sensitive observers, the clarity of their vision complemented by the sweet precision of their prose. Even so, their lives diverged drastically in 1920. Unlucky Babel was eventually devoured by the revolution he had helped to sustain, whereas his fellow Odessan blossomed in the New World. This is not to say that the decision to emigrate had been taken lightly or easily. The aftershock must have reverberated for years, and it can hardly be coincidental that Neider's first novel (a product of the Eisenhower years) details the near-intolerable pressures on a man—much like his own father—forced to choose between his wife, who dreams of an American renaissance, and his mother, fiercely determined that her favorite son should remain with her in Akkerman. Neider Sr.'s judgment was wiser than he knew. Had he surrendered to his mother's importuning he and his dependents would have shared her terrible fate.

The White Citadel startled and delighted its early readers. It astonished them because it examined the conflict between husband and wife (not to mention that between mother and son) with a rare—almost Strindbergian—intensity; it astonished them because this couple, presented with no exotic flourishes, were urban, middle-class, Bessarabian Jews, a social group hitherto underrepresented in American literature. Saul Bellow, fresh from translating

Isaac Bashevis Singer, and therefore familiar with the more folksy inhabitants of the Polish *shtetlach,* was one of the novel's admirers, along with Thomas Mann and E. M. Forster. "I was fascinated by your book," he wrote to its author (soon to become a friend). "It amazed me that you should have such recall of the Old Country." And Bellow was right on the mark; the novel not only details the inner and outer lives of its protagonists, it also contains vividly sensual descriptions of the landscape, of the estuary, the limans, the vineyards, the Black Sea beaches. Bellow's praise carries another implication: *The White Citadel* is—if not autobiography—at least autobiographical.

As it happens the tormented couple—Kostya and Tanya—do have a young son, Petya, a good candidate for the author's alter ego. The book ends with all three (plus Tanya's stylish father) en route to America, burdened with baggage, literal and metaphorical, both in their arms and in their psyches. It is to the place they have left, to Akkerman, that Sid Little, a dapper American in his autumn years, returns in "The Left Eye Cries First" (just as Charles Neider did in 1989 when Mikhail Gorbachev was still president of the Soviet Union). It would be unnecessarily reductive to maintain that Sid Little is Petya grown old and that both are representations of Charles Neider, for there is much in both books that is fictional, but it is surely of some significance that the pair share the same childhood memories, or (more accurately) that Sid Little remembers things that have happened to Petya, things that are described in *The White Citadel.* And so having crossed the Iron Curtain (as it then was), Sid Little remembers being undressed by his Nana, a peasant girl, who mocks his diminutive member and, noticing the blushing boy's interest in her vast bosom (stuffed, it seems to him, with feathers), brazenly bares it. He remembers his hatred of *penka,* the loathsome skin that floats on the surface of overheated milk, and the occasion he threw a fit of hysterics rather than eat the stuff. He remembers vacations by the Black Sea; being coated by his father with dark, stinking mud; being in a carriage that spilled its occupants. All of this may make "The Left Eye Cries First" sound like an elegy, a return to origins, a closing of the circle. It is hardly that, however; it is, if anything, a gesture of renewal. Sid Little commences his odyssey immediately after his second bar mitzvah, itself an optimistic gesture, another act of renewal; a fresh start even. Neither Little nor Neider is ready to call it a day just yet. On the contrary, the novella is a testament to Sid Little's extended run of good fortune, which he accepts gratefully, always aware of the proximity of its corollary; fatal illnesses strike close friends, and the malevolent demons still resident in the land of his birth turn a fellow traveler's vacation into a tragedy.

Even luckier than Sid Little is Joel Stevenson (another alter ego; Neider is himself a Fellow of Stevenson College, part of the University of California at Santa Cruz), who visits the White Continent, rather than the White City, only to become the sole survivor of an air crash. Stevenson's other claim to immortality is that he's the hero of one of the first American novels to be set in Antarctica, a rival claimant being Edgar Allen Poe's Arthur Gordon Pym. In any case, *Overflight* is certainly the first written by someone with an intimate knowledge of the place. "'Lord, Lord,' I kept saying to myself," Neider writes in *Beyond Cape Horn: Travels in the Antarctic* (its beautiful nonfiction precursor), "'how lucky I am to be here,' and my eyes filled with tears." Why the tears? Obviously Neider was grateful to be one of the few nonscientists to appreciate the awe-inspiring beauty of the scintillating landscape, but he was also mindful of a more specific lucky break; being fully aware that had his father decided differently it would have been the fire, not the ice. "My paternal grandparents, elderly people in Bessarabia, who had refused to flee the town of Akkerman because they were unable to believe the stories of German atrocities," he adds, "had been locked in a synagogue together with other Jews and been burned to death."

There was, perhaps, yet another reason for the tears; maybe Neider knew that he had found *l'endroit juste,* as Babel had done, the place where he could test himself under the most stringent conditions, the place where he could be a man among men, the place where he could confront life's polar opposite.

It is possible to be precise about the moment Neider came face to face with death in Antarctica; on January 9, 1971, the helicopter in which he was a passenger crashed on the inhospitable slopes of Mount Erebus (which, incidentally, conceals one of the world's three fire lakes in its crater). The quartet within all survived the impact, but found themselves stranded at an altitude of 12,200 feet. The temperature was –31 degrees Fahrenheit. Survival rations were in short supply. The four men huddled in a tent designed for two. For ten hours their lives hung in the balance, until they were finally spotted by a helicopter and rescued. "*That* brought me close to the heart of the continent," notes Neider wryly, "too close, perhaps." It was also the launching pad for *Overflight*.

There's a full-length photo of the author (a self-portrait) on the back of that novel's dustjacket. Neider is sporting a black coat and shades. His arms are flexed on either side of his body. He looks as he must have looked all those years ago, when he practiced his quick-draw technique in front of a mirror. This is not inappropriate. Indeed Neider has thanked Antarctica for, above all other things, having granted him the opportunity to "come to grips with an almost untouched literary frontier," the Wild South, so to speak. It is the location of the borderline between civilization and the wilderness, between rationality and madness, populated by latter-day badmen and Cossacks; transients all, the maverick seamen, the daredevil pilots, and the shaggy-haired scientists.

It may be a bit hard to believe but this weather-beaten gunslinger's first published book was actually a psychological study of Franz Kafka, which he called (with uncanny prophetic powers) *The Frozen Sea*, extracted from Kafka's aphorism, "a book must be the axe for the frozen sea within us." Nor is its title the only link between the budding literary critic and the experienced traveler. According to Neider's interpretation, the eternally frustrated hero of *The Castle* is a scoptophiliac, a voyeur or compulsive observer. It is this obsession with the surface of things, this refusal to break through into his own subconscious, that denies K. entry to the holy of holies, to the place of ultimate revelation, the heart of the eponymous castle. Having already been too close for comfort to Antarctica's all-consuming heart, N. is unexpectedly offered a second peek; he finds himself enticed by the local sirens to enter the frozen sea and is tempted by the "pure glasslike quality" of the water to remove his clothes and jump in; his body literally aches to be immersed in this "soothingly cold liquid."

It is a decisive moment, when Neider must determine what sort of writer he wants to be, whether to opt for revelation or observation. He wisely plumps for the latter, preferring to celebrate the world rather than his inner space. It is what he was born to do, his eye being a precision instrument, a God-given Leica.

The benefits are apparent in his wonderful descriptions of the White Continent, which turns out, on closer inspection, to have a far richer palette. "The ice isn't just white," writes Neider, "it's full of pastel subtleties: rose, pink, prune, pale green—and then suddenly electric, cobalt blue. And the textures are infinite: ripples, waves, soft ice, crevasses, hummocks, a variety of snow covers." These vivid descriptions are augmented, in *Beyond Cape Horn,* by exquisite photographs taken by Neider himself with man-made equipment. He is also responsible for the image on the front cover of *The Grotto Berg*. It appears to show the forehead and eye sockets of an ice-giant, slowly emerging from the blue water. The berg seems to stare at the reader, at the same time drawing the reader into its dark vacancy. . . .

It is no surprise, then, that the hero of "The Grotto Berg," George Barber, is a photographer on assignment to study and shoot the Southern Ocean. This he does from the decks and bridge of an icebreaker (an axe to the frozen sea), despite the apparently inexplicable hostility of its captain. Although a seafarer, Jack Tourneau resembles nothing so much as the weak (and probably corrupt) sheriff of a small town in the middle of nowhere, unsettled by the arrival of a stranger. To Tourneau, Barber's cameras are as threatening as a pair of revolvers; they are disinterested witnesses that will record all his faults, despite his best efforts to hide them. And what are these faults? The greatest is undoubtedly his femininity (unacknowledged to his conscious self). Perhaps this is why he is so hostile to Barber. As primitives are said to believe that the camera will steal their souls, so Tourneau may fear that the camera (which so often fetishes women) will inevitably reveal what he has been trying to hide (not least from himself) for so long; that he is not a man among men. This version of femininity as the feared terra incognita within finds its most vivid expression in the Grotto Berg itself. Indeed the tale's tragic climax is provoked when Tourneau steers his ship into its dark cavity (supposedly for Barber's benefit). Theirs, needless to say, is an unnecessary conflict; Barber is no spy and has no bone to pick with Tourneau and his cronies. His only concern is embracing the alien world without the ship. He is, for example, far more interested in the mysterious beauty of a huge berg that reminds him of the Sphinx. So captivated is he that he photographs it compulsively. One of the results (or something very similar) may be studied in *Beyond Cape Horn.*

Even so, Barber is not the narrator of "The Grotto Berg." The role is filled by Hank Elkins, member of a three-man Antarctic Observation Team. This bifurcation, this forking of the self, enables Neider to be, simultaneously, both the observer and the one who enters the Grotto Berg itself, who eventually penetrates the heart of darkness. He has thereby solved the dilemma he faced on the strand of the frozen sea: whether to take the plunge, and how to record it should it prove fatal.

This duality also serves to utilize and reconcile Neider's twin heritage. On the one hand there are Babel's men in extremis; on the other there is the more democratic (or American) battle of wills between an outsider and a powerful incumbent. In "The Grotto Berg" the man in control happens to be the captain of a vessel tossed by the alien winds of the Southern Ocean, which immediately links the protagonists to their great ancestors in Anglo-American literature; Coleridge's Ancient Mariner and Melville's Captain Ahab (to name but two). A lineage that certainly does not embarrass Neider.

Such risky feats of self-discovery would be remarkable at any age, but in an octogenarian they are almost superhuman. What drives him is his inexhaustible curiosity. Visited by prostate cancer he immediately becomes an expert and produces a manuscript on the subject that is more travelogue than medical textbook, with Neider as a pioneer, a scout sent ahead to map out the unknown territory. Recently Neider sent me a photograph that could have been mistaken for the fizzing heart of Mount Erebus. In fact it was of Baltic amber (a small part of a small piece), about 45 million years old and containing insects. Neider, however, was less interested in portraying fossilized mites than in revealing the fairyland world within, which (he added), "I deal with noninvasively (that is, optically)." That old eye of his remains interested in everything, from whole continents to microscopic worlds within ancient sap. And it still sees what most others miss. Call him Hawkeye.

CLIVE SINCLAIR
June 2000
St. Albans, England

THE GROTTO BERG

ONE

I had gotten to know George Barber, a nature photographer, in Christchurch, New Zealand, where we had shared a motel room in a quiet neighborhood after a flight from California, via Samoa, in an Air Force C141, the Starlifter. He was about my age, turning forty. The intensity of his brown eyes reminded me of Picasso's, yet he was quiet, softspoken, at times almost shy. He was on the tall side, had light brown hair prematurely graying at the temples, attractive features, and a prominent Adam's apple. He was lean, wiry, muscular, yet, oddly, could have passed for a scholar, an academic. I liked his musical voice with its touch of a drawl, and his dry, intelligent, quietly ironic manner. He was married, childless and lived in San Francisco.

The water heater in our room had inadvertently been set to produce steam, and Barber barely missed scalding himself as he twisted the handle the wrong way to turn the shower off. Was this an omen? I would later have cause to wonder about it, because during the upcoming icebreaker voyage he would sometimes appear to be on a death-defying mission. We bought a first-aid cream at a pharmacy downtown near the cathedral, which he applied on the burned places.

And now we sat next to each other on the flight down to Antarctica in a Navy Hercules, the work-horse plane, with its four turboprop engines, its silvery pylon tank under each wing, and with its capability of lifting off on wheels and landing on skis. All the Herc's seats were occupied. The plane was too crowded with clothes and baggage for much moving about. A young crewman handed out pink plastic earplugs. I squeezed and inserted them. They slowly expanded in my ears but I could still hear a loud roar, occasionally punctuated by hissing. The engine noises were so great that when I unplugged my ears for a try at chatting with Barber I soon felt at risk for a free tonsillectomy. The variations in temperature were crazy, as a guy proved with a small thermometer he had brought with him. They ranged from 55 degrees to 120 degrees Fahrenheit. A cockpit crewman said a circuit breaker had gone bad and that it couldn't be replaced at this time.

People reading, sleeping. Several playing bridge. One civilian's head shaven except for a crewcut scalp lock. A stout young Navy woman horsing around. Aft, a mountain of baggage strapped and chained down. Barber peed into a little aluminum funnel while standing precariously on the baggage, his privacy partly shielded by a plastic curtain.

We managed the midday meal, a great event because it broke the flight's eight-hour monotony, by balancing it anxiously on our laps and proceeding with the careful, tiny gestures of brain surgery. I buttoned up and fell asleep. When I awoke, sweating profusely, we were flying over a white, cottony world that hurt my eyes when I tried to observe it through one of the few portholes, but it apparently didn't trouble Barber, whose Picasso eyes, also unprotected, and giving the impression they were enamelled, were fixated on the remarkable world out there.

People crossed themselves as we passed the Point of Safe Return—meaning that beyond this point we had insufficient fuel to return us to New Zealand and that we had to continue toward Mc-Murdo Station on Ross Island come what may. The bolts on the plane's naked walls, icing up, had turned white. Everybody donned polar clothes as we prepared to land, so we were sweating as we touched down bumpily on skis. We taxied for what seemed a long time on the ice of Williams Field. Having had tail winds, we arrived an hour early, at 5:00 P.M. McMurdo time. McMurdo's time was the same as Christchurch's. It was now January, and Christchurch, on daylight savings time, was eighteen hours later than New York and twenty-one hours later than L.A. McMurdo in summer had round-the-clock daylight. The station was eight hundred and forty nautical miles from the Pole. The sun moved counterclockwise, at McMurdo dipping by midnight. At the Pole it didn't dip at all.

We were hit by bluish polar sunlight on leaving the craft. Barber and I had been here separately before. Standing on the ice of Williams Field and staring at Mount Erebus, we were momentarily bewildered. Barber said he felt he had lost something in not arriving slowly. "You move so fast it takes you time to catch up with yourself." Vast, white Erebus, an active volcano, beautiful, large, pure, majestic, and only one of three on the planet to contain a red-hot lava lake in its crater.

We had a hard, bumpy, tracked-vehicle ride on the Ross Ice Shelf. On land we transferred to a heavy truck, which dropped us off at the Chalet in McMurdo, a wooden building in the Swiss style, where we received our room assignment from Harry Easton, the McMurdo rep (representative) of the National Endowment for Science. Easton, tall, cool, long-haired, was new to us both. He had a tiny mouth, like a dash, an odd feature in so gangly a body. I didn't notice its size when it was open, so was it the lips that were tiny? Did such a mouth mean something? Nature? Nurture?

I could still hear the painful thunder and feel the massaging vibrations of the Herc. I remembered the gentle, swaying trees on the River Avon banks in Christchurch, and the heat rising off the tarmac at Harewood Airport. McMurdo Sound, which I saw from a window, was frozen, but the Chalet felt toasty, even a little overheated. Easton looked authoritative in it, as if he had spent several austral summers here, though this was his first.

"If sunspot activity doesn't hold up their flight in Cheechee, Paduani and Markovsky will arrive day after tomorrow," he told me.

Sunspot activity, by affecting the earth's ionosphere, could severely disrupt radio communications in Antarctica. Cheechee was a code name for Christchurch.

Ben Paduani and Peter Markovsky were my colleagues on the three-member Antarctic Observation Team. We were scheduled to go to the Antarctic Peninsula, where we would visit a number of foreign Antarctic stations to check for possible violations of the Antarctic Treaty. In two or three days we would board the Coast Guard icebreaker PENGUIN, demilitarized for Antarctic duy, for the thirteen-day Southern Ocean voyage to the Peninsula. The PENGUIN was currently breaking ice in McMurdo Sound several miles north of McMurdo. George Barber would join the ship too. However, whereas the Observation Team would have a vacation while on the PENGUIN, Barber would photograph aspects of the ship and the Southern Ocean.

As Harry Easton reached for a sheet of paper on his desk his head entered a shaft of brilliant sunlight that burnished his straight blond hair, revealing single, streaked, golden strands. For a moment I had the illusion he was a woman, an image shared by Barber, as the latter told me in our quarters that evening. Surprising me, and causing me to wonder about his sexual orientation, George Barber also told me it would be interesting to shoot a section of Easton's hair up close, and that he could imagine the composition and colors of the finished 11x14" print.

Easton's hair brought Wild Bill Hickok's to mind. Poor Wild Bill, who, like Barber and me, had been in his fortieth year when he was shot dead in the back by a drunken coward in the Number Ten Saloon in Deadwood City, Dakota Territory, while playing poker, holding a pair of aces and two eights, unable to draw to a full life.

"What if Paduani and Markovsky are delayed?" I asked Easton. "Will the PENGUIN leave without them?"

"Not to worry," Easton said.

"You can hold the ship for them?"

Easton replied with a little shrug, which I assumed meant he had a certain authority over the ship's movements, at least in the McMurdo region. Again a motion of his head caused strands of hair to glow.

I don't remember why, but he mentioned some odd behavior by Jack Tourneau, the PENGUIN's captain. On going ashore by helicopter for a first look at McMurdo, Tourneau had loudly stated that the amount of litter at the station was "a disgrace" and that a number of the station civilian personnel were "lazy and incompetent." He had also publicly called the U.S. Antarctic program "a civilian boondoggle." And there had been a flap between him and Easton because Tourneau had refused to manifest George Barber on the PENGUIN for the Antarctic Peninsula area without rewritten orders from Easton, calling Easton's current orders "too damn vague." Also, he had referred to Barber as a "freeloader."

"What's between you and Tourneau?" Easton asked Barber. "He bristled at having to take you to the Peninsula." Easton pronounced it Peninshula.

"Don't know the guy," replied Barber, frowning.

"Why did he call George a freeloader?" I asked.

Easton shrugged. "I know this," he said. "If George is a free-loader, so is Jack Tourneau. So are most of us down here. But please don't quote me. I have a very full plate. I don't need to add to the flap he created."

"But why did he pick on George?"

"If I knew that I'd be a genius."

McMurdo's black hills and roads gave the station the look and feel of a mining camp. Porous volcanic rock everywhere, crushed to gritty dust in the lanes. Meltwater rivulets, running down the hills, crossed the station on their way to McMurdo Sound. Strong smell of diesel fuel. Smell, taste and feel of volcanic grit in the intensely dry air. Clouds of earth dust from noisy, heavy trucks passing nearby.

Barber and I were to share a room. It was on the ground floor of a rectangular two-story building sitting on stilts to avoid heavy buildup of snowdrift. Two single beds, two closets, two red arm-chairs, an overhead light, a floor lamp, bed lamps, a coffee table, a linoleum floor and steam heat. I thought, "Cool. I'm on Hut Point. Robert Falcon Scott lived a little way from here in mighty different style." We made up our beds, washed up and strolled toward the en-listed men's mess for dinner.

"Sure you don't know Tourneau?" I asked.

"Positive."

"So why did Easton ask what's between you and Tourneau?"

"Don't know," said Barber, shaking his head.

"Tourneau's a jerk."

"Or a trouble maker."

Soft, evening light. Lilac-washed sea ice. Light blue sky. White and Black Islands showing icecliffs. The beautiful Royal Society Range in the west, beyond wide McMurdo Sound. A red-painted Coast Guard cutter with white superstructure and high radar and other towers, squatting on the scarred ice of the Sound. It was the PENGUIN. Who would have imagined the events that would soon occur on it? Certainly not I—Hank Elkins, D.C. bureaucrat with the resonant baritone.

We ate near some young men with long, untamed hair, indiffer-ently washed sunburned faces and hands, brown or blond beards, and dirty, baggy clothes. Five Kiwis with flowing hair, heavy beards, heavy dusty boots, plaid woolen shirts, brown tweed trousers. Jokes and laughter. A young Kiwi woman was explaining to one of them that she was a graduate student in biology, studying parasites in Antarctic cod and trying to culture them. We took long, absorbing looks at the several women present, knowing there would be no females on the icebreaker journey and few women on the Antarctic Peninsula, where we were heading.

I recalled being stunned by the sight of real live females the last time I had left Antarctica, landing in the heat of Christchurch. And stunned by *green grass* and by *little* people (kids) and by *trees*. I remembered an Antarctic joke. A couple of helicopter pilots brought an artificial Christmas tree down from Christchurch and planted it in Wright Valley, one of the deglaciated Dry Valleys. Flying some greenhorn civilians on a brief tour, they pointed out the tree far below as an example of extraordinary and still-unexplained Antarctic life-forms. They pulled it off with straight faces, and with riotous laughter over bourbon in the McMurdo wardroom afterwards. Meanwhile the visitors, still awe-struck elsewhere at the station, felt graced to have witnessed the miracle. O ye little fishes, how I loved Antarctica and its wild jokes, some, like the treacherous weather and the even more treacherous ice (not least the snowbridged crevasses and falsely solid-looking bergs), unplanted.

We returned to our room and turned in, grateful to whoever had rigged cardboard blinds that reduced the fierce light seeping through the drawn red curtains. The low-hanging sun shone like a spotlight. Scientists coming and going, some preparing to go into the field, others impatiently waiting for delayed cargo. During the night I was vaguely aware of helicopter sounds, winds, voices, door slams.

* * *

For Barber there was trouble on the PENGUIN from the start. There were six of us guests on board: the three members of the Observation Team, two young ornithologists from Point Reyes, California (called birders on the ship), and Barber. However, whereas five of us were quartered in Temporary Officers' Quarters (TOQ), Barber had been assigned to Chief Petty Officers' Quarters (CPOQ) even though there was no shortage of space in TOQ. The five of us were shepherded politely by a lieutenant senior grade down below to our quarters, but Barber was led through what felt like a maze of old-time steerage to *his* quarters by a large, overweight, overbusy, frowning, coughing chief petty officer named Bob Flynn to the darkness of Flynn's own rack, where Flynn pointed to the rack above his, growled "This is yours," and abruptly left.

No matter that both sets of quarters were on the same deck, one below the wardroom. They were worlds apart in several ways, as Barber soon learned. Compared to his quarters, those in Temporary Officers' Quarters were almost elegant, a fact painfully visible to him, for he had to pass the TOQ whenever he went to and from the wardroom or the bridge. The TOQ racks were wider, had no ladder and pipes for occupants to contend with, had chests of drawers for clothes and were well curtained for privacy. We other guests had each other for company when relaxing away from the wardroom, whereas when Barber wasn't in the wardroom he was the sole civilian in a nest of military men.

It was impossible for him to socialize in CPOQ, because as a civilian he didn't have the liberty of the CPO lounge, with its huge color blowup of a HUSTLER centerfold: a spread-eagled blond young woman wearing high black boots, pubic hair shaved, open vulva gleaming with oil. At times, feeling he was being observed with intense curiosity (possibly mixed with hostility) by the indigenous occupants of Chief Petty Officers' Quarters, he wondered if they suspected him of spying on them.

The TOQ had a temporary feel, like hotel or motel rooms, so a visitor felt comfortable in them, whereas the CPOQ had a feeling of permanence—they were people's homes at sea, where Barber could easily feel he was trespassing and where he had to behave cautiously, if only because there were always people asleep there, day or night, which was why the sole source of light was the red bulb over the head's door. Some of the men didn't trouble to draw their rack curtain. Others, like Barber, lacked one.

Barber didn't care to ingratiate himself by flicking on the overhead light, the only general light available. At times he could vaguely grope his way by the red light, but sometimes, for reasons unknown to him, this light too was off. He was helped by a tiny flashlight, made in France, he had brought along, whose rays just barely showed him the way. But often, finding himself without it, he had to grope to keep from bumping into things. Inside the head the light was blinding.

His rack was located at the end of a dark corridor between rows of racks. The corridor was so narrow he had to navigate it sideways to avoid brushing against curtains or, God forbid, human bodies. There was nothing to sit on except the deck. To reach his rack he had to climb a narrow metal ladder with rungs that were little more than toeholds. Some of the ship's plumbing (massive pipes, some insulated, some bare) threaded its way in several levels just above the length of his rack, so it could be hazardous to sit upright suddenly, a fact he learned the first night on board when he slammed his forehead against hot metal, which disoriented him for a couple of hours and caused him to resolve never again to wake up bolt upright.

He had no space, covered or otherwise, into which he could put his clothes when he removed them, so he hung the hangable ones from the cold pipes. For his shoes, watch and other small items, he made use of the dusty top of an adjoining metal cabinet, which someone else was using for a similar purpose. A lot of this Barber did by feel, for, unlike the other rack lights in CPOQ, his wasn't working.

The temperature of his quarters was curious. There were times when he was reminded of McMurdo's sauna, and he understood then why some of the crewmen, not one of whom he ever saw wearing pajamas (they slept in their underwear), didn't draw their rack curtain. Mostly he felt he was in the tropics, except for the times when he half froze.

Once, he was standing on one foot while removing a boot. Suddenly the ship lurched severely and he was flung into the curtained rack on his right, which turned out to his intense embarrassment to be occupied, and by Chief Bob Flynn. Flynn usually kept his curtain drawn, whether he was in the rack or not.

The large-bodied chief, who had been lying down, sat up, glared at Barber as the latter disentangled himself, and growled angrily, "What the hell's going on?"

Barber mumbled an apology and an explanation as Flynn slowly, angrily and skeptically disappeared behind his curtain.

On another occasion, when Flynn was absent, Barber was again thrown into Flynn's rack, this time as he was preparing to climb the steel ladder to his own rack. Surrounded by curtains, Flynn's rack was like a tiny room. Barber saw pinups on the rack's ceiling, snapshots of a naked young woman with outspread legs. "What's all this about pinups?" he wondered. "What's the point—when there are no women around? Why make themselves even more horny than they are? Is it to remind themselves they're heterosexual?"

* * *

The assignment of his rack bewildered and humiliated Barber. He felt singled out for derision—here, take this crazy CPOQ rack and shove it, you're not good enough for officer quarters. He recalled how differently he had been treated the previous year on the DECEPTION ISLAND, another Coast Guard icebreaker, when that ship had cut a channel in McMurdo Sound. The channel made it possible for resupply ships to service McMurdo in the austral summer. McMurdo Sound was deeply frozen during winter. He had been assigned a cabin adjacent to the captain's, had regularly dined with the captain at the latter's invitation, had used a desk in the captain's cabin at the captain's insistence, and had shared the captain's head. The captain, a gentle, reserved, softspoken man with a thoughtful air, had offered Barber a tour of the ship and had placed the ship's helicopters at Barber's service whenever they weren't in official use. Unlike Barber, the captain didn't cotton to Antarctica.

"Look at those mountains," he said. "Nothing but ice. You can't profit from it. If we drilled for oil I'd understand why we're here. It's different in the Arctic. I don't get it. I find it hard to understand why anybody would want to come back here. But you hope to, right?"

They were standing on the bridge. The ship, heading south toward McMurdo, was cutting a channel in McMurdo Sound, the ice of which now, in the austral summer, was about six feet thick.

"I can't get enough of this place," said Barber.

"Different folks, different strokes."

A little later a couple of crewmen said in Barber's presence they hated skuas because skuas attacked Adelie eggs and chicks. One, on a lower deck, cast a line overboard, meaning to fish among a group of skuas scavenging the ship's garbage in the channel. A lieutenant junior grade, standing near Barber and aware of the captain's liking Barber, leaned over the gunnel and said, "I don't think that's a great idea." The crewman reeled in his line and disappeared.

What did Barber's rack assignment mean? I recalled Easton's saying Tourneau had complained Barber was a freeloader, and asking Barber, "What's between you and Tourneau?" Why was an unobtrusive, affable guy like George Barber, a nature photographer with an excellent national reputation, being discriminated against? And by whom? By the captain, Jack Tourneau himself, with his small head, curly reddish hair and girlish hands?

Understandably, Barber and I became increasingly aware of Tourneau, especially at the abysmal, ancient movies in the wardroom each evening. It was strange to see Tourneau enter the wardroom briskly while all stood at attention, walk rapidly to his captain's chair and sit bad-postured like a smug adolescent. His loud, vulgar laugh exploded regularly during the films. He felt free to do that, as if he was showering his officers and his civilian passengers with lordly gifts. Lapping up the movies, he laughed his head off, destroying the little gray matter in it. His guffaws at the cheapest gags were echoed by his stooge, Lieutenant (senior grade) Sonny Peterson, the young operations officer with the poker back and the soft, large ass that threatened the seam of his Coast Guard trousers.

Tourneau and four or five cronies, Ben Paduani always included, played poker nightly on a round table at the aft end of the wardroom, two players occupying the long wall bench and Tourneau invariably using a captain's chair, his back toward Barber and me, as if to underline the message that he was deliberately ignoring us. We usually hung out at the dining table. He ignored *me* only when he saw I was in Barber's company. His back was small, and his hands were small and feminine, with nails that were far too pretty for a seagoing military man. And he wore a striking ring on his left pinky, which Paduani told me was a one-carat Burmese ruby flanked by two small diamonds. The mounting was massive: twelve pennyweight of 22K yellow gold, with a circular stripe of 18K white. White bezels surrounded the diamonds, a yellow bezel the ruby. Loving poker, Barber wondered if Tourneau and company were playing stud or draw, and what the stakes were, and if he would be invited to join the game. Poor Barber, how innocent can you be? After all, the captain refused eye contact with him, and had him live in a kind of steerage while voyaging on the world's worst waters. It made me think about Barber. Spit in a guy's eye and he thanks you for the moisture.

It could have been argued that Barber's rack was a temporary situation and that one should be careful not to make a typhoon out of a squall. But we were scheduled to voyage for almost two weeks on the PENGUIN in the world's notoriously most turbulent waters. Furthermore, being quartered in CPOQ inevitably caused a psychological distance between Barber and the other guests, myself excepted. In essence, though like the rest of us guests he had officer rank while on the PENGUIN and therefore hung out and dined in the wardroom, he lived with the chief petty officers. Because I had grown to be very fond of him, I took a particular interest in his odd circumstances. I asked a number of people why Barber was being quartered in CPOQ. They didn't know.

Barber had a fine sense of humor, which could easily be directed at himself, so the comic side of his situation was by no means lost on him. Still, it graveled him more than I expected, causing me to wonder if there wasn't also, under his balanced, cool, calm, scholarly demeanor, a paranoid streak. And I kept being made aware of the intensity of his Picasso eyes, which belied his otherwise calm, mild, almost academic expression. It was strange to me that this exceptional talent should occur in such a mild person. Was there another, explosive side to him?

TWO

Our first few days at sea were the subject of jokes. There was almost no wind. At twilight the lower sky turned indigo, suggesting a requiem mass. Upheaved floes were yellow with plankton. Lightning spears of electric green showed in the ice cracks. Some of the horizon bergs were chalk-white, others were turquoise, amethyst, candy blue. One berg suggested a skyscrapered city made of cake frosting.

Then we got some swells, and the orange wardroom drapes began to pendulate, and we heard tales of fifty-degree rolls the PENGUIN had taken coming down from New Zealand, and of the captain's being unable to sleep and eat, and we wondered if they were exaggerated and, if they weren't, when *our* sea luck would run out. Barber wondered what would happen to his work when the weather soured and the weather decks were secured and he'd have available only the crowded wardroom, the crowded bridge and his crowded rack.

The sole roughness in the ship's movements at this time was due to our ice-breaking, but it could make for quite a rough ride. The prow rammed and climbed onto the ice with a great growling, snarling and hissing. The hull roared as the larger ice chunks scraped against it. Descending the ladder while the ship lurched heavily seemed hazardous enough to warrant moving in slow motion, with a wary eye on the heaving steel deck. We were sailing on waters frigid enough to kill you by hypothermia within ten or fifteen minutes if you fell or were thrown into them.

But the usually tempestuous Southern Ocean was suggesting a Mediterranean calm. The sky serene, pale blue, pale green, with a trace of apricot at the horizon. The ocean deep blue, in places verging on black. Our wake a broad, frothy, creamy, golden highway. A killer whale's head, like a dark bullet, thrusting up out of an ice crack. The snow petrels, with their softly white bodies and black eyes, were shy, ghostly, hauntingly beautiful, fast, and hard to shoot against snow and ice. At times Barber thought they were an illusion. The presence of birds helped humanize these very high latitudes for him.

Now and then the sea was littered with ice bits that seemed to be remnants of an ice explosion. Our prow swept them effortlessly aside. Creating gorgeous satiny swells, we came to ice pancakes, some with a solitary seal. Dreamy scenes peopled by ghostly white and bluish ice shapes. Fissures verging on cobalt. Water the color of blue ink, with a scattered layer of mercury. A rising wind shivering the sea. The icefields were summer-thin on this ocean surrounding the sole pulsating continent. During the austral winter Antarctica greatly expands in size because the sea freezes for hundreds of miles outward from its coastline. No ship can penetrate the ice then.

* * *

One morning Barber and I were alone in the bow. The ship was in a field of white, glary pancake ice. Some of the pieces had vivid blue miniature cliffs. The prow sounded harsh and metallic as it struck ice. When it hit ice that was quite thick it rose high, swayed and shuddered. I enjoyed the feeling of riding onto a floe, cracking and splitting it, or with a faint swishing sound knifing our way through gently heaving pack. Occasionally we rode up onto an ice island without cracking it and had to veer away, leaving some of our red paint on the small inlet we had created. Masses of heavy pressure ice lay directly ahead, upraised, irregular. Breaking our way laboriously through it, we took a beating.

The thinner pack ice looked rotten. The sky flamed golden. Rosy bergs in the distance. Mincke whales blowing. The sea full of restless silver coins. Far away on the left a thin, horizontal ribbon of burning platinum seemed to be shouting "Light! Light! Above all let there be light!" And huge light rays were blasting seaward from the upper sky roiling with dark, purplish clouds. All this weathered, colorful ice, and some embayment cliffs resembling crumbling Roquefort. A berg lunging upward like a huge wing. Soaring muscularity, yet fine too in the details (engravings, scratches, embossings). The water ahead of us was shouting "I'm the most electric blue on the planet!" Barber imagined we were sailing on a molten jewel.

* * *

Awaking in the middle of the night to go to the head by the light of the faint red door light and his little French flashlight, descending his vertical, steel rack ladder carefully and, with uncertain footing passing sleeping bodies and being startled by the head's blazing light, Barber felt the throb of the icebreaker's engines, heard the loud scraping sounds of the prow breaking ice, and sensed the ship's pulsing life and his unfamiliarity with everything. Yet he was happy, because the inaction of Christchurch and McMurdo had turned to action. He was *on board*, voyaging on the fiercest, most remote, most unpredictable, most fascinating and, not least, most beautiful vast body of salt water on earth.

He had quickly learned how to move readily from his rack to the door leading to the steep steel stairs that ascended to the wardroom deck, how to get from the wardroom to the ship's prow on the same deck, and how to go to the hangar deck aft, where he could jog or walk, or to the forward deck between the bridge and the wardroom deck. Because the gunnels were very low, he was aware of how easy it would be, if the ship were rolling heavily or the decks were icy, to fall overboard, and of how little hope there would be of a rescue. He was also aware of how much steel there was in the form of hatches, decks, stairways and stanchions, and of how injurious a fall could be. Later, when the weather was rough, he was often alone on deck for varying periods of time, photographing. If he had been swept overboard he wouldn't have been missed for an hour or more.

I was greatly impressed with his almost fierce dedication to his self-imposed task, with his equally fierce, almost fanatical, self-discipline, and with his love of nature. He never talked about what he was doing or planned to do, he just *did* it. Among the guests only he and the young birders had tasks. He easily worked as hard as they, and with much greater danger to himself. Actually, there was no danger at all in their job, because they worked only on the bridge.

Barber was most likely to feel the bite of the polar air in the bow, but it was wonderful to be there, with no human artifact to spoil his view, with the illusion of being solitary, yet with the comforting sense of the ship's power beneath and behind him. In the bow he felt superstrong, as if he himself was moving ice islands, probing for leads, shattering floes. He was free of the funnel exhaust, and was in greater motion than elsewhere on the ship as the bow rode up onto a floe and slowly cracked and split it, or moved through and beyond it, out into a snake-like lead suddenly, surprisingly, temporarily free of ice. He glimpsed electrifying turquoise colors when the ship exposed submerged ice. Riding in the bow felt at times like voyaging in a fairy tale.

* * *

Joining me one afternoon on the fantail deck, where I was idly studying the ocean with Ben Paduani and Peter Markovsky, he asked quietly, "Hank, any idea why I was assigned to CPOQ?"

"*I* understand a military head? *Hey!* I'm a middle American, a civil servant, and a bureaucrat."

"Bureaucrat?"

"One of the noble ones. Have you thought of mentioning it to the CO?"

"He refuses to have eye contact with me. So does Peterson, the operations officer. And Carpenter, the executive officer, just barely manages to meet my gaze."

"The CO has a hair up his ass. He's been at sea too long, breaking too much ice and wind."

"*If* the CO is behind your rack assignment, he may have meant to do you a favor," said Markovsky to Barber. "He may have assumed you want to get a feel for the crew instead of being out of touch up in officer country."

Markovsky, born of White Russian grandparents in Yugoslavia, had certain meticulous habits, such as the way he lit his pipe, using a gold Cartier lighter. When he wasn't playing solitaire he spent much time reading papers that he removed from a Mark Cross leather attaché case. He dressed expensively. In D.C. and Christchurch I'd sometimes find myself admiring his London shoes. Although he spoke with a foreign accent, he had an easy command of English.

"Then why didn't he tell George so?" I said. "Why does he avoid eye contact with him? And why didn't he welcome him aboard?"

"A CO's reasons are often not obvious to those below him," said Markovsky, shrugging.

"What's the beef?" Ben Paduani asked Barber aggressively, surprising me. "What does the country get out of your being here? You're lucky to be on board."

Paduani, out of line, deserved a forceful rejoinder. But Barber, smiling, merely shrugged. I was disappointed.

Paduani was a lieutenant commander in the Navy and a poker buddy of the CO's, so he was likely to see things from the CO's point of view. He was usually cool toward Barber, as if he had adopted the CO's bias. He was trim, taciturn. Smiles didn't come easily to him. His laugh was forced, emerging in brittle, staccato explosions. On the PENGUIN he always wore Navy greens in contrast with the Coast Guard khakis.

"Improper question, Ben," I said, thinking "stupid question." "The same could be asked about us. We're getting a long and paid vacation."

"One that's developing problems for me back in my office," remarked Markovsky drily.

"The helo pilots dislike Tourneau to a man," I said. A helicopter in American Antarctica was called a helo, pronounced heelo. "They say the CO despises them because they have no duty when they're at sea. They're not scouting for leads or helping to break open a channel. Or ferrying crew between ships or between ship and shore. They read, shoot the breeze, play cards. So he ignores them or acts contemptuously. It gravels him because they're not under his direct command. The pilots like George. Roger Dove, the PENGUIN's senior pilot, a lieutenant commander, makes a point of calling George's attention to any unusual ice formations."

To Barber the helo pilots of the DECEPTION ISLAND had been as exotic as their ship. He had flown with them high and far on a couple of occasions. As the helo soared above McMurdo Sound he had belted himself to a long heavy canvas strap hanging from the ceiling. The strap allowed him to stand at the very edge of the open cabin hatch while shooting. He saw at a glance the ship, the ice beyond it, and beyond the ice the far-flung western mountains. The perfectly mirrored ship, trailing a series of ripples, was sailing on burnished clouds. It looked like a pretty toy sitting on sea ice marked by ripples, cones and something resembling pebbles. The ice had the color of old ivory. The ship's smoke cast violet shadows onto it. Leaning out of the hatch, looking straight down, he shot black-and-white ice patterns—rectangles, triangles, ellipses, ovals. The wind rushing into the cabin was very cold. Closing the hatch, he rubbed his hands together until they were ready to function again. Returning to the ship felt like a bird returning to its nest.

* * *

Our hull was red for vivid contrast with ice. Wearing a red parka with the hood down, Barber was shooting from the bow, using two black, sleek 35mm cameras hung around his neck. Paduani, Markovsky and I, also wearing red parkas, were sitting nearby on the deck, backs against a metal wall. Paduani, strong, straight-postured, was reading a paperback. He rarely chewed the fat, always wore a Buck knife on his belt and, if the deck was sunny and the sea smooth, could usually be seen reading huge, cheap paperback novels, powerful legs outstretched, solid meaty back against a bulkhead. Ballpoint in hand, Markovsky was working on some notes. He was a solitaire addict who fondled cards in the wardroom even when the wired-down chairs and dining table lunged, as later often happened, and the cards threatened to take off and fly around the room.

The two young birders were using binoculars on the bridge. It was said they had great sea legs, a real compliment on the Southern Ocean, especially on an icebreaker, a vessel without a keel, built like a football: if you roll twenty-five degrees to port, you roll twenty-five to starboard. They were logging the kinds and numbers of birds the ship would encounter during its very high-latitude Southern Ocean traverse: albatrosses, Antarctic petrels, Wilson's petrels, snow pigeons, occasional Adelie penguins on ice floes, and the like.

They were also noting any seals, crabeaters mostly, and whales they spotted: fins, blues, Minckes. They kept to themselves even after wardroom meals and rarely laughed or engaged in chitchat with the rest of us guests. They acted as if only *they* had a dedicated mission in life, because only *they* of the people on the ship were making a contribution to the world's knowledge of the Southern Ocean bird biomass. They were on the bridge or the bridge wings in all weather, staring at the vast reaches of oceanic space. They worked around the clock, sometimes together, at others spelling each other.

* * *

The world was in riot. Nature had exploded. The Southern Ocean felt endless, and the flying birds seemed trapped in our gravitational field. This ocean had such exotic features that Barber sometimes thought he was imagining them. Lavender sky, wine-blue sea. An albatross abreast of us: great wings, with tips upturned. Barber was mesmerized by the sea birds, which seemed mysterious beings from another planet, and shot frames, frames, as if film was free. I wondered what he was seeing and what the finished product would be like. An amateur photographer, I sometimes would ask him photographic questions and was impressed with his precise, uncondescending, generous replies.

Sometimes we'd spot a huge berg at a great distance and, fascinated, would watch it grow as we neared it. The presence of ice in any form helped give us a sense of our forward motion. Unless we stood on the fantail and studied the wake, or in the bow, staring at the spray, it was hard to sense that motion. At times Barber felt becalmed, and a desperate, trapped feeling would cry "Help! There's too much water! And too much space! I'm in danger of spending an eternity in it!"

* * *

An ice wasteland, and the PENGUIN forcing a lead to spread open: a blue river snaking across a white plain, the lead's icy underparts glowing blue-green. White pancake ice stretching to the horizon.

Sometimes we cracked it but mostly we shoved it aside. No sign of life aside from the ship. What did we have to do with this alien world? Yet the meeting of forces, ship against ice, was hypnotizing. And then we saw three Weddell seals on a floe, dark cigar shapes humping toward a lead. And a Weddell on the starboard, upraised on its flippers, staring at us. Brownish-gray back, gray chest and belly, black chin. And two Adelies staring at us while standing on an ice floe. Beyond a lake-like stretch of water a solitary Adelie walking energetically on a floe. Seeing us, it dove into the sea and swam madly to escape us, breaching rapidly. Several Adelies ahead. Three tobogganed to escape us, others ran frantically, white rumps, black backs. Then all tobogganed.

* * *

There were two sittings at meals. Mine and Barber's was the early one. Tourneau's, at which he was rarely present, was the later one, so Barber was spared having to observe him accidentally while dining. Meanwhile Barber worried about his five cartons of equipment, which had been deposited in the aerologic office, whose door was often left ajar, to his surprise and irritation. What if somebody were to break into them? What chance would he have to retrieve stolen goods? The icebreaker was as complex as a village.

He had finally, after several persistent requests to Chief Flynn, been assigned a locker in the bank of lockers near the CPOQ head. The locker was lockless, but he had luckily brought along a combination lock. Though the locker wasn't spacious enough to hold his cartons, it adequately contained his parka, anorak, some extra clothes, his cameras, some film, photo notebooks and a journal. His suitcases were stacked on top of a large metal cabinet near TOQ.

One evening Sonny Peterson, the captain's stooge, the young, vain, officious operations officer with the short blond hair and big ass, was presiding as usual at the head of the table. He was generally silent during meals. Barber was reminded of a chief warrant officer on the DECEPTION ISLAND who also presided at dinner, but in a predictably foul-mouthed way. He too had a fat ass. Peterson's language was super-clean, as if it was attached to his ramrod back.

Turning suddenly to Barber, he said, "Can I ask you a personal question?"

"Okay," Barber responded after a slight pause, looking surprised, fork in midair. I was fascinated by his strong Adam's apple.

"One of the enlisted men on the bridge reported that you carry a tape recorder in your shoulder bag. True?"

Barber almost always wore a leather-and-canvas shoulder bag with a broad canvas strap, whether he was on land or at sea. I had grown accustomed to seeing him with it in Christchurch and Mc-Murdo. I had assumed he used it to carry extra film, lenses and so on. Peterson's blunt question, almost aggressively put, was a public invasion of Barber's privacy and implied that the supposed contents of Barber's bag were proof of sneaky behavior.

There was a moment when Barber wanted to say, "Who *are* you, with whom I've hardly exchanged a word, to ask me such a question? Or did Tourneau put you up to it?"

"No," he replied quietly, his strong, wiry hand holding the fork clenching. "But if I had one in my bag I wouldn't use it in the presence of other people without their permission. I have a recorder with me but I haven't broken it out of its carton since I packed it in the States."

He had spoken softly, in measured tones, looking only at Peterson. I empathized with his indignation and admired his self-control. But, studying his several, straggly, prematurely gray eyebrow hairs (he was only just turning forty, as I noted earlier), I almost wished he would threaten Peterson with the fork.

"We understand your Arctic book has real dialogue," continued Peterson, "so we assume you used tape recorders to record it."

"I keep a journal and photographic notes. I try to make the entries as soon as possible. When I used a tape recorder it was only for interviews. I never used it without permission."

"We also understand you put four-letter words in the mouths of people in your Arctic book. What if their moms read that stuff? It would shock *our* moms if you reported *our* use of four-letter words."

People laughed. I guffawed.

"I suspect there are few *moms* who haven't been exposed to four-letter words, which are hard to avoid even on TV these days," somebody said, and that closed the episode and left Peterson glancing around the table uncomfortably.

After dinner I said privately to Barber, "Peterson's a shit. I'm surprised you didn't blow your stack. I would have. I wonder if there's a connection between his confronting you like that and your being assigned to CPOQ. I doubt he has the balls unless the CO's encouraging him."

Barber responded only with a smile. What was holding him back? Why was he taking all the crap being dished out to him? I was beginning to feel embarrassed being known as his friend.

THREE

The weather turned rougher and the air grew bitter as we came into full contact with the prevailing, unopposed westerlies that spin around the globe, often reaching the peak of their intensity in the funnel of the Drake Passage. The ship's gyrations caused my heavy clothes to rub unpleasantly against my body. Now there were no large western landmasses to shelter us. We were voyaging eastward on a great-circle route south of the Antarctic Circle. The Furious Fifties and Roaring Forties were far to the north. We had entered the atmosphere of the Southern Ocean, soupy by contrast with that of continental Antarctica.

Recalling the hauntingly blue polar sky, I thought of crystal days in the Dry Valleys and remembered the cruel sunlight at the Pole, where the sun, so low above the horizon, and biting through thin, dry, superclean air, could hit you like a third-degree spotlight.

We were hugging the edge of the ice pack south of us, which dampened swells and subsided high seas. Roger Dove, the senior helo pilot, told Barber that the CO tried whenever possible to avoid rough seas because of his weak sea stomach. With the weather cold and wet (hail, snow driving into our faces), the decks slippery, the hatch doors heavy and ready to slam against our hands, we tended to stay in the wardroom, where we sometimes watched the ship's TV program, mostly run by enlisted men. The program, offering news, interviews and skits, elicited ironic or sarcastic comments by the officers.

We rolled endlessly. We sometimes also pitched and yawed. The wardroom's main, long, rectangular table was bolted into place. The chairs were wired down. Behind the starboard orange drapes was a metal wall. Had the chairs on that side been free to move about, a person sitting in one might have gone careening backwards against it. The table had a fiddle, a low railing around its perimeter, to keep plates from tumbling into our laps, but still we had to be careful about navigating food.

The drapes served as fairly good inclinometers and were sufficiently inaccurate to generate a variety of dogmatic opinions about how far we had rolled. Using them together with arcane formulas (I had majored in math at college), I computed the rolls and offered the wardroom the results in what I have more than once heard described as a deep, resonant, loud voice. Some of us, like Barber, avoided this exercise, believing it merely promoted seasickness.

Being physically inactive made Barber very tired. Whenever possible he ventured out onto decks that were wet and tilting or littered with snow or hail, where if he didn't hang onto something with a solid grip he might head for the gunnels and possibly be unable to stop himself from going overboard. He was aware of how low the gunnels were. The water's temperature was about 30 degrees Fahrenheit, lower than that of freshwater ice. The water would immobilize him quickly, then rapidly kill him with hypothermia and/or drowning. With the water so turbulent, there was little chance of his being spotted, even if someone saw him leave the ship.

"You're pushing your luck," I once remarked to him.

Smiling, he shrugged. His lean face, with its attractive smile lines, had a two-day stubble. "What's the alternative? It's what I love to do," he said.

To have called him brave would have been questionable. He did what he needed to do, was *driven* to do. It was a job like any other, the performance of a duty. Yet despite such reasoning I tended to romanticize him, to see him larger than life, certainly larger than any other life on board I was aware of, and infinitely larger than Tourneau's.

The hatches he had to pull or shove open were heavy, and the ship's heavy rolling and pitching seemed to make them intent on amputating a hand or leg. As he fought with them it seemed questionable, at times, as to who was shoving whom. Out on deck he soon began to feel frozen and mesmerized. On returning to the warm wardroom he felt sleepy, relieved and vaguely irritable, as if unfair demands had been made on him.

At times he felt the ship routines were brainwashing him, causing him to do things he normally would avoid, such as sitting through stupid movies that seemed like Large Events because they were ordained in some way. Uniformed men gathered each evening as if for a serious colloquium. Chairs were arranged just so, one always being reserved for the captain, who made a formal appearance while everybody rose. And the film did its duty in the little projection booth.

The weather turned still rougher, but though the air grew bitter, it was exhilarating. The winds were very strong. Birds kept their distance from the ship, possibly because they didn't dare risk being blown against it. On the weather decks there was now too much seaspray for normal cameras, so Barber began using two waterproof ones, which he could rinse off under fresh water when necessary. He spent a good deal of time keeping his equipment in shape and writing up photographic notes. Intrigued by the weather and the birds (albatrosses, Antarctic petrels, an occasional snow petrel), he frequently got very wet out on deck. Even on the fantail deck, which was more protected than some of the others, he had to brace himself against objects during the times when, shooting, he couldn't hold on to something.

* * *

One day after dinner Barber and I went to the "phone shack" in the bowels of the ship for phone calls. The phone shack was very hot. The ship's main winch had broken. Two men were working on their knees to fix it. The large wire panel protecting the high-voltage section had been removed.

"Don't back into that, it's live," warned Chief Bob Flynn, who to our surprise was the phone operator.

Our backs to the high-voltage section, we waited in line for our turn. I reached my wife, Leora, at home in D.C. The connection at first was very poor. Her voice sounded fantastically treble, like a singing canary's, then resembled my baritone before settling down. It was around 3:00 A.M. her time. Her nickname was Leelee. We had two daughters, ten and twelve. She still wore a protection cord around her neck, which she had worn when I first dated her.

When I met Leora she had a private income, was a painter and lived in a canyon in southern California. Her house and studio were at the north end of a former ranch, close to a live oak with a nest of yellow jackets. Nearby was a flaming jacaranda. Beyond the studio was the stony, usually dry creek bed, a great deal of scrub and some live oaks. The air in the neighborhood smelled of eucalyptus leaves.

The place contained old corrals, cottages, tack rooms, stables, barns, and was complete with live oaks, cypresses, eucalyptuses, pepper and jacaranda trees, rattlesnakes, scorpions, black widows, a couple of bobcats, a mountain lion and huge, night-strolling tarantulas. Some of these creatures lived in the canyon itself, others in the tangled-underbrush green mountains that loomed over it, cutting short the morning and afternoon light. Except in summer, when they came down to the creek bed, looking for water, the rattlers generally stayed away from the canyon floor. Mostly I'd find them sunning individually up on the high, dry fire road open to the brilliant sky. The black widows kept to themselves in the cool darkness of the decaying haylofts.

On occasion, when I was bored, I'd shoot a .22 target pistol into the nest. The yellow jackets would quickly spot me as the evil one. Waving my arms over my head, I'd race into Leora's house, slam the door shut, run into the bathroom, observe in the mirror the several yellow jackets that had followed me inside, and kill them serially with a bath towel. My activities never seemed to disturb her when she was painting, which made me wonder just how seriously she took her work. On the surface she took it very seriously.

Eyes glowing, she used to say she loved living in the canyon. Loved the flowers (poppy, sticky monkey flower, geranium, ice plant), the silences, the olive trees, the orange and lemon trees, the gnarled live oaks, the powerful-smelling barns (ancient hay, rotting wood, greasy leather), the feeling of being hugged by mountains.

"Hey! How are you?" I said on the icebreaker in my heartiest voice.

"I've taken up belly dancing," she announced.

"Oh?" I said, thinking of her fat portfolio and the fact she'd never had to work for a living.

"Don't sound like that. It's an authentic art form."

"Really?"

"Absolutely."

Leora had a way of saying "absolutely" which reminded me of one of our early dates.

"By the way," she had announced, "I recently had an affair with a twenty-one-year-old guy. He betrayed me."

"Really?"

"Absolutely. It was painful. I've had many profound affairs lately. But brief. We were in Pamplona for the running of the bulls and I lost him in the crowd. I searched for him for two hours, then returned to our hotel and lay on the bed. He came in and said he had drunk too much wine and had had sex with a woman on some vestibule stairs not more than fifty yards from where he had disappeared. The bulls had been running, and he and the woman had jumped into a doorway, had found themselves alone in the dimness and had had sex. He said it was trifling, an accident, nothing more. I was very angry and very hurt."

In those days her idea of flattering me was to say, "You're not easily replaceable."

Lying in bed, observing her, I would think, "She bought those tight-fitting, expensive dark trousers to show off her beautiful ass to younger guys."

Leora was impotent as a painter, couldn't finish a canvas, invariably hit a block. She claimed this was due to her never having been taught composition, an excuse I didn't encounter until we were visiting the sprawling ruins of Volubilis on a height in Morocco.

"Those Bennington shits! Never once mentioned composition!" she said in a poisonous tone.

The ancient Roman mosaic floor looked faded in the fierce sun. We had been having rainy weather for days but today the Morocco sky was naked. Pompeii, Vesuvius, Mount Erebus. Among the ruins Leelee looked skinny. Thin naked arms. Naked ladies in the mosaic floor, one riding a horse. A satyr-like beast, with a horse's body in back and a man's naked torso up front. Sex implicit in the Roman floor, but not between Leora and me in Morocco for days. She was in one of her frenetic moods that could last for a couple of weeks. She opened a jar of tap water she had brought along at an American friend's suggestion and sprinkled it onto the floor to make the colors glow. The floor ran with blues, grays, reds.

"No no!" cried an elderly Moroccan caretaker, joining us with surprising agility. We hadn't noticed his nearby presence. He wore a blue caftan and a faded gray cowboy hat like one out of an old John Wayne movie. Had John Wayne given it to him? I had read somewhere that John Wayne had shot a film in Morocco.

"This is not permitted!" the caretaker said angrily, glaring more at me than at Leelee.

"Why not?" Leelee asked abruptly, dismissively.

"A historic ancient monument! Cold water—hot stones—they crack!"

"Nonsense. It's good for them," she said with a hint of hostility. But she closed the jar and replaced it in her brown Gucci shoulder bag.

"Ugly American," I thought I heard him mutter as he retreated to his post.

Had he heard John Wayne say that? Leelee had made no eye contact either with the caretaker or me during the incident. Her fat portfolio gave her great assurance during such moments abroad, even in Morocco, where the U.S. had a military base in Kenitra and where she felt she could buy her way out of most anything.

Driving the borrowed new red Volvo station wagon, we looked briefly at Moulay Idriss, a mountain village behind Volubilis, then stopped for half an hour at a primitive souk outside another village. Mud. Smells of incense, herbs. Fast drive through lovely countryside to Kenitra because we were due at 7:00 for a promised elegant dinner. Bad smells, as of sewage, outside the Kenitra house. Dali and Picasso lithographs on the walls, and a French journalist, doubling as an art dealer, showing lithographs for sale. Leelee bought two by Picasso. She despised Dali, whom she considered a slick showoff.

She had been kinder to cockroaches in the canyon than to me.

"Please go away! Don't you see you're not wanted?" she had cried at them when they appeared on the walls, usually while we were dining. After all, they were God's creatures, like herself, a Tibetan Buddhist. They were hard of hearing. Her tolerance of them made my muscles twitch.

She still banned terms of endearment in our relationship. The most passionate thing she ever said to me was "I care about you," in a pensive tone. But was she ever jealous, particularly of an English woman married to a Moroccan. This was at a party in Kenitra when the lady, whose husband was away, showed too much interest in me.

Leelee's guru, also married to an English woman, made dates to sleep with his female idolators, who jostled competitively to make long-in-advance reservations for assignations with him. He had a cottage near his Big Sur house that he used for his transfiguring one-night stands. She got her wish and spent a night with him. He never wore a watch, a habit she imitated, so she was a doozy to travel with. Lived in a state of transcendental timelessness.

"I've been doing prostrations since you left," she said now.

"How many?"

"I've done thirty-five thousand. I have to complete fifty by the end of the month."

"How many a day?"

"Four hundred. You begin and end with a standing position. You drop to your knees on a pillow, stretch out, stand up. My goal is a hundred thousand. There are also mental exercises but I'm not allowed to talk about them."

She got on the subject of her Aunt Stella, a child molester, a rich, divorced, childless resident of San Francisco who had died about a year ago.

She said, "I first found out about her when John, my brother, was eight and I was ten. He walked into my bedroom and said that Aunt Stella was pulling down his pants and sucking his cock, and he seemed not quite sure how to deal with it. Was it all right? Was it not all right? I was astounded."

"So what did you do?"

"I didn't know how to deal with it directly either with him or with Aunt Stella, so I went to Mother, who as usual was in front of her mirror. I told her what John had told me, and Mother did not look at me. She continued to brush her hair and said she would deal with it. And that was that. Mother had beautiful, long brown hair and knew it. Eventually I found out she did nothing.

"Many years later I questioned John about Aunt Stella. At first he denied anything had ever happened, but then he said it had happened many times and that he had eventually gone into counseling with his wife because it had led to problems in their marriage. I don't know how child molestation affected his marriage. I imagine it could alter the sexual expectations. Perhaps, for instance, there was a bond established with the molester, almost like a satanic bond, that the wife isn't allowed into."

"So then?"

"So then I confronted Mother. I said, 'Don't you recall I told you?' And she denied ever hearing about it. My parents were still on friendly relations with Aunt Stella. There were holiday visits, birthday cards, as if nothing had ever happened. I told Mother it was outrageous that no one had ever confronted Stella, because a lack of confrontation was a way of saying to John, 'There's nothing wrong with this.'

"Mother said, 'Where do you get these ideas? The women's movement?'

"I was shocked. I found out afterwards that my parents took action, confronted Stella and severed relations with her. Father said, 'It's in the past. Let's forget about it,' and he said it in a way that suggested 'It's not that important. People make too much of it.'"

"So when did you find out you might have been involved with Aunt Stella?"

"Not for a long time, because I had almost no memories of my childhood, and I still don't, as you know. John, two years younger than I, will tell stories about what we did as kids, but I have no recollection. I can remember, though, in vivid detail the tastes, smells, texture of a cousin's house in Monterey, where I would go as a little girl. I can remember the swing, the dandelions in the lawn, the boar's head and golden drapes in the living room. Yet I can't remember the house I grew up in. I can't remember anybody else's house. I can remember stepping on a bee when I was about eight. I can remember the ice cream truck. But I don't remember people. I don't remember experiences, places.

"It wasn't until after Stella died that I got a call from Patricia, the executor of Stella's estate. Patricia said she had found photographs of me in Stella's files and that Stella *was* a child molester and that John was not the only victim, there was a whole string of them, Patricia included. And she had every reason to believe that I was one of them, because of the way Stella had talked about me and because of the photographs."

"Were any of the photographs pornographic?"

"No. Patricia told me that when Stella fondled her she would start to shake, her face would get very red, and her hazel eyes would burn. John never described such a change, but then maybe she was different with boys."

I recalled our earliest days together.

"I'd like you to fuck me," Leelee had said one night when, preparing to go to Ethiopia, I was feverish with typhus and other shots. She was beautiful, sensitive, with beautiful legs, hazel eyes, long brown hair, and lovely breasts that had several strong dark hairs growing around the nipples. The hair embarrassed her but not enough for her to have it removed. In the early days, when I first did oral sex to her, I was surprised to discover she had a strawberry tattoo on her right thigh, close to her crotch. In the uncertain light I mistook it for an unfortunate birth mark.

"See the strawberry?" she asked.

"What is it?"

"A tattoo."

"Why'd you do it?"

"When I'm old and my flesh sags, it will still be young and fresh and will remind me of my mortality."

Admiring her candor and boldness, I had convinced myself she had infinite credit with me. When I was inside her that very first time (in her canyon house; there was a mandala on the wall above our heads; it was raining), she cried, "You're breathing wrong!"

"Okay, I'll breathe with one nostril."

A melodramatic silence.

"Would you like me to leave?" I asked.

"It's raining too hard."

"So lend me an umbrella."

"I want you to stay."

"And stop breathing?"

"You're not funny."

I had thought, "Why spoil my fun just because she's odd," and continued making love.

She had a great body. I used to get a kick out of her stunt of standing in front of me stiff as a board and falling backward with a Mona Lisa smile, trusting me to grab her delicate wrists at the last possible moment. She was small and light enough to get away with it, otherwise we would have both fallen. She was beautiful in a haunting way. Her face reminded me of Virginia Woolf's. And she enjoyed sex, though she had a Lawrentian hangup about coming simultaneously, as if without it sex was tragic.

"*I'll* get on top," she'd say. "And don't you dare come before I say *COME!*"

And she'd ride me, monitoring our progress, and would get touchy if I came too soon. She laughed triumphantly at the Holiday Inn in Marrakesh when, she claimed, we absolutely, to the split second, came together.

She wasn't a cool travel companion in a country like Morocco, where she often claimed some young guy had surreptitiously felt her ass or stroked her long brown hair in a marketplace. Once, in an almost empty first-class compartment between Kenitra and Marrakesh, she complained that a middle-aged army officer was staring at her, and asked me to tell him to stop. I finally sat down opposite him and gently explained in English that my wife was afraid of the evil eye, and would he kindly not look at her directly. Instead of being offended, he took a liking to me and we had a pleasant chat, ignoring her.

We had had a layover in Casablanca of an hour and a half, during which Leelee couldn't go to the john because men, naturally, had commandeered the ladies room. Theirs had gone bad, with water running out all over from under the door. We had been entertained by a one-handed, red-headed little boy, a jester, a peddler of cactus fruit. Leelee gave him a handful of change, which he deftly pocketed in his ragged pants. She was finally able to pee in our first-class car. She had a wonderful, flexible bladder, could go for hours without a problem.

Black tunnels, no lights, pitch black in the train. Desert scenes, adobes, sheep, solitary shepherds.

In Marrakesh she insisted we stay at a little inn in the crowded medina, the native quarter, "to get a feel for the people," forgetting it was hard to do it in a town as touristy as Marrakesh. I preferred to get a feel for the Americans in the Holiday Inn in the area of the wide European boulevards. But as usual she prevailed. Winston Churchill, who liked doing watercolors in Marrakesh, would have taken a dim view of our inn. I think Leelee hoped to emulate him in that town and medium but never got around to it. She didn't get around to a number of things, including, on occasion, sex with me for weeks at a time.

Next morning she said she was very tired and needed to sleep in. After a native breakfast downstairs I walked aimlessly in the neighborhood. Returning to our room, I found her crying. She was still lying in bed. Her beautiful eyes were very red.

"What's the matter?" I asked.

She wouldn't say, but from her dark glances I quickly got the idea I should be feeling guilty. There were times when I was sure she hated me because she thought I was more gifted than she, yet I had made absolutely no effort to be an artist. As Freud said, who understands women? Finally she said she was very upset because she had botched a pencil sketch of a man in the inn's restaurant last evening.

I was reminded of two things. During a mobbed exhibition of drawings by Leonardo at the British Museum, she had situated herself in front of one and had laboriously tried to copy it. It was a piece of American rich-girl insanity. That evening, after Leonardo, we dined in a so-called French restaurant near St. Paul's. She had coq au vin, I had pigeon. Her poor bird, black meat with black gravy, was accompanied by soggy old potatoes and wan carrots. My pigeon wasn't much prettier. I ate half of it. Only great gulps of red wine saved me from upchucking.

Studying her plate with moist eyes, she put her fork down and, staring at me as if begging for first aid, said in a quavering voice, "I feel pathetic."

"How come?"

"I haven't had a good meal."

It didn't help that I was in a jolly mood. I loved the comedy of it, being taken by the "French" restaurant. We left soon after. I bought a bottle of scotch at a pub.

Lying on the bed in our plush hotel room, Leora wept bitterly, much as she did in the woebegone Marrakesh room. I tried soothing her by pointing out it was only a lousy London meal, but she cried as if something much more important was involved. I was sympathetic, empathetic, outgoing, funny, but she never gave me a clue. Meanwhile many sips of straight scotch wonderfully settled the pigeon in my tummy.

Back to the medina room. She finally composed herself and had a bite. The day started to clear, get hot, but soon clouded over. We went to some souks. We had a fight during a late, bad lunch at a nondescript hotel. We took a carriage ride to a park and back. Lightning, thunder, huge gray clouds. In the evening, in our room, lying down, she wept hard again and refused to go to the nightclub where we had reservations, or to dinner elsewhere either. She said she was very frustrated and unhappy but didn't explain why. I took a walk in the medina. We barely spoke to each other when I returned dinnerless to the room.

At last she said bitterly, "I'm very disappointed in myself."

"Why?"

"Don't you see I tagged along in Europe and North Africa and did mostly your thing instead of mine?"

"I thought all our travel decisions were mutual."

"On the *surface.*"

"Oh come on."

"Forget it."

As I started to drift off to sleep I had a sense our relationship had peaked. Wrong. That was before we even had kids.

I got up at 6:00, saw it wasn't raining, conferred with her, and we decided to drive to the Ourika Valley. We were both eager to see some countryside, take our attention off ourselves. The day was too cloudy to let us have views of the high Atlas Mountains but we saw some of the lesser ones. In a Berber village we were besieged by kids begging us to buy amethyst geodes. She gave them some money without buying any. We were in a completely changed mood when we returned to town. That was when we gave up getting a feel for the people and moved to the Holiday Inn, where we had what was, in her opinion, one of the finest simultaneous orgasms ever, one which however, in *my* opinion, I performed on command.

I don't know what there was about Paris that fired her up against me. There was always something askew when we were there together, even when we didn't stay in the Latin Quarter. I remember the first time we were in that town together. She was there a couple of days ahead of me. I joined her after some business in London and Helsinki. We were walking along a street at night, when floodlit Notre Dame came into view amid the ooze and swish of traffic.

"Surprisingly delicate edifice," I said.

"It's auspicious for your Paris stay."

"What?"

"Your enjoyment of Notre Dame. It's a good beginning."

Since she knew I had visited Paris a number of times, her remark was too heavy a psychological load for me to deal with, so I dropped it. I have occasionally wondered if I should have dropped her too. She was manic, distracted, a cold fish sexually in Paris and Madrid, where she often complained she wasn't seeing enough in the museums, as if I was personally responsible. She seemed to hold me accountable for a lot of things. During a night in Barcelona I told myself she wasn't well, she was disturbed by visions of all the paintings she had seen and not had time to digest. I resolved to husband her strength.

She had a habit of angrily or playfully slapping me sometimes, or punching me with her small fists. It goes without saying I never hit her back. One night, in a Latin Quarter hotel—we hadn't had sex in quite a while (in my opinion)—she struck me in the face.

"That's it," I said. "I'll take care of myself sexually the rest of the trip and find another sex partner on my return to the States. We can finish the trip as travel companions."

"I'll stay in Paris. I won't go with you to Spain and Morocco." She had never been to either place.

"Fine."

I went to the single bed beside two street windows and tried to sleep. Our room was on the second floor. Noisy young people outside seemed to be shouting in my ears. They didn't abate until around 1:00. Toward dawn I saw she wasn't asleep.

"A longish stay in Paris won't be good for you," I said. "You'll miss too much by not seeing the Prado. The Goyas are breathtaking."

"I can go to Madrid alone."

"Come there with me. I'll hate it there without you. I'll hate Barcelona and Morocco and all. Please."

"All right."

"I love you," I said. Which was true. I also admired her.

I didn't believe either of us knew on what basis we would continue together. But we had a pretty good time afterwards, with a day in Grenada for her to see the Alhambra.

* * *

I talked a while longer with her on the icebreaker. By the time it was Barber's turn he had changed his mind. Maybe he was turned off by what he had heard, though he hadn't heard Leelee's side. It would have been no sweat to guess she and I weren't exactly suited to each other. There are all kinds of relationships. It all depends on how much you can take. And for how long.

And yet it was a relief to communicate with Leelee, however oddly. I felt more fully human after the call, and more relaxed and cheerful. After all, I had been in contact with the temperate region. I recalled the so-green trees on the River Avon's Christchurch banks.

Barber never mentioned his wife to me. I wondered what kind of lady she was. Helpful? Broadminded? Had she generously given him the liberty of Antarctica? How old was she? Why were they childless? Were they considering divorce? I was disinclined to ask probing questions. By now I liked him too much to risk diminishment.

"Bob, mind if I snap a couple of shots of you?" he asked.

"Be my guest," said Flynn, surprised.

Barber shot several frames. We returned to the wardroom and played poker, Barber continuing to teach me the game.

During a break in the game he reached into his shoulder bag and brought out several Antarctic rocks, which he placed on the wardroom table. He collected Antarctic rocks, and had with him on the ship some he had found recently in the McMurdo region. One he called a ventifact, an artifact made by the wind, a piece of dark gray, oval-shaped basalt resembling a beautiful work of art, maybe by a sculptor like Noguchi, who loved working in stone. He said the upper surface of the rock had been exposed for centuries to the prevailing westerly in Taylor Valley, one of the so-called Dry Valleys.

This westerly, he explained, was a katabatic (gravity-caused) wind roaring down, past icefalls, from the polar plateau, the vast, dome-shaped ice mass that in places is almost three miles thick and at the approximate center of which were the Pole and Pole Station. Using particles of ice and dirt, the wind had carved the rock sinuously, streamlined it, and had darkened and glazed the top surface so thoroughly it looked oil-wet. He said the streamlining informed you of the rock's orientation in the valley. The under part of the rock was unremarkable looking. He said the valley was flanked by Alpine glaciers tonguing down mountains to the valley floor, and that the floor, snow- and ice-free in the austral summer (the Dry Valleys had deglaciated long ago for reasons still not well understood), exhibited an astonishing variety of rocks: basalt, sandstone, scoria, granite, slate, marble, chalk, whathaveyou.

He pointed to a round, ivory-colored geode whose upper surface, covered by rust spots eaten into the stone, resembled a furry jaguar skin.

"I wonder if ancient seaworms carved the spots," he said.

He held up a rim-glazed double-concavity piece of sandstone.

"This is an ashtray rock from Windy Gully, near Terra Cotta Mountain," he said. "I wonder what chemical and mechanical processes, working over what stretches of geologic time, formed these cavities."

All the rocks had a powerful, acrid seasmell, stirring memories of kelp, iodine, chemicals. Some had salt crusts.

FOUR

B y now, at times, we felt we were on an interminable voyage to nowhere. We were as far from help by air or sea, if it were urgently needed, as it was possible to be on the planet. We were making one of the highest-latitude traverses of the Southern Ocean ever, hugging the pack ice that rings Antarctica in the austral summer, because the captain, O Captain, had a weak sea stomach, and pack ice had the virtue of calming the fiercest seas in its vicinity.

The complete, total, absolute absence of women, old or young, married or single, plain or beautiful, bright or dull, charming or deadly, military or civilian, feminist or otherwise, in a ship full of horny men helped sustain the illusion that we were lost in outer space.

* * *

One afternoon we were proceeding slowly through fog, a white, cottony shroud, flirting with the possibility of slamming into a massive piece of low-floating, very dense ice, the kind known as blue ice, which could be so hard you needed a jackhammer to work it and which could damage even an icebreaker. Barber and I, standing in the foremost part of the bow, were peering into the gloom when a phantom ship emerged slowly from the veils and with it the wavering strains of Russian folk music. At first, incredulous, we thought we were being spooked by that wild ocean.

The weather decks quickly became crowded with onlookers. Markovsky said it was probably a Russian whaling factory ship violating the international treaty regarding the harvesting of whales. Tourneau tried to contact the phantom ship by radio. No response. He used light-signal calls. To no avail. Veering, the phantom slipped away into the fog like a guilty thing, its music trailing after it.

Leelee was a great believer in signs and portents. If she had been on board she probably would have predicted an exotic, bloody tragedy for us. Why not? She feared fog, and lived in a foggy spiritual state much of the time, in my opinion. Though I considered myself a rationalist, at times I fell under her spell and accepted as gospel things I later called nonsense. Now, on the icebreaker, on the gorgeous Southern Ocean, about a million miles from nowhere, I felt an uncanny shiver course through me, as if my spine was warning me that something terrible was about to happen.

Assuming Barber to be as rational as myself, I was too embarrassed to mention the feeling to him. Which was just as well, for I increasingly sensed a nascent tenderness verging on love in my regard for him, which surprised me. It would have been a pity to mar my relationship with him by seeming kooky.

The Russian ship brought to mind Coleridge's Ancient Mariner, who spots a phantom ship on which stern-faced Life and grinning Death roll the dice to see who wins him. And I remembered reading a tale about a murder being committed on a ship on the Southern Ocean, and a plague like AIDS attacking the crew, officers included, and all ports brutally turning the ship away. And I recalled the legend of the Flying Dutchman, in which a stubborn Afrikaner sea captain, a murder having been committed on his ship, vows he'll round the Cape of Good Hope during a fierce storm or be damned. Damned he is, eternally doomed to beat against the wind while trying to make Table Bay, Cape Town's harbor. His phantom ship, the FLYING DUTCHMAN, is believed by some seamen to haunt all seas, especially the Southern Ocean.

That same day, when the fog lifted, we saw small, intensely blue bergs with pinnacles, turrets and marvelously rounded forms that made Barber think of medieval castles. And we came upon a berg, rising like a pyramid, that reminded him of the Giza Sphinx near Cairo. The face, staring in profile, was grim. Its tight lips reflected great pain. Its lower lip trembled with emotion. Its mouth was slack, as if in dismay. A chunk of raw flesh hung from its cheek.

He kept photographing it from various angles with several lenses. As we moved closer he imagined the head had once been face down, chin at water level, mouth and nostrils barely able to breathe, and that now the face was suggesting horror so great as to distort baboonish features until they became nightmarishly human. He hoped to suggest in photos what he was imagining.

That night he dreamed he was back at the Black Lagoon, ghostly, phosphorescent, near Ushuaia in Tierra del Fuego. He had been there the previous year after crossing the Drake Passage from Antarctica in a wooden motor sailer. In Christchurch I had been powerfully affected by some of his Tierra del Fuego pictures, but especially by his Antarctic ones in a large-format book I had bought in Christchurch and which I had with me on the PENGUIN. Rotting Black Lagoon tree stumps in smoky water. Thick bogs friendly to a minute, insect-eating plant. Trees covered with large, green-yellow balls of a parasitic mistletoe. Tree stumps on naked, stony banks. Tangled, jagged, bleached gray trees, all branchless.

And then he dreamed the sphinx berg's mouth was grinning malevolently at him. He awoke frightened, with a rapidly beating heart.

* * *

The weather grew fiercer, so fierce that the weather decks were secured, the hatches lashed, and there was nowhere for Barber to shoot and nowhere to kill time except in his rack or the wardroom. The latter was more crowded than ever. No views of decks or ocean. We might as well have been in a submarine, except that a submarine's decks are placid, whereas ours constantly heaved. Much playing of solitaire or listening to news on the ship's radio station or to the crew's radio programs. The constant heavy rolling, yawing and pitching tired everybody physically. Like me, Barber was growing lethargic from too much food and was irritated by lack of space, lack of privacy and by incessant indoor cigarette smoke and outdoor diesel exhaust fumes.

He wondered anxiously what his cameras were missing. He needed to go to the bridge but was reluctant to do so because Tourneau still rigorously avoided eye contact with him. Once, visiting the bridge briefly, he was made to feel unwelcome—not verbally but by silence and body language—by Sonny Peterson, the man whose posture was exaggeratedly straight, as if he had poker back. Tourneau wasn't on the bridge.

On his second trip to the bridge Barber was immediately approached by Peterson, who was frowning heavily, almost scowling.

"Mr. Barber, you'll have to leave," said Peterson. "This is a restricted area."

The birders were on the bridge despite the heavy weather. The place Barber had taken for granted now looked precious to him. His work *needed* it. Would he have to fight for it? Given where we were, it was unlikely the weather would relent for quite some time. Without the freedom of the weather decks he was cooked.

"I have legitimate business here," he said quietly.

"What business, sir?"

"To study the Southern Ocean. What about these guys?"

"Sir, I have specific orders to give them the liberty of the bridge."

"Lieutenant, it's part of my project to study and shoot the Southern Ocean in all weather," said Barber, still quietly. "With the weather decks secured, I can study and shoot it only from here."

"Sir, you'll have to take that up with the CO."

Saying nothing more, Barber returned to the wardroom, feeling guilty for some reason, and angry about the feeling, and angry in general. He was aware that some of his anger was caused by the foul weather, his current lack of exercise, his increasing sense of physical confinement, and by the persistent effects of the ship's motion, which made all parts of the icebreaker seem to be fighting him in a cunning and potentially deadly way. Oddly, Tourneau's authority on the ship, even though it didn't embrace Barber in any important way inasmuch as he was a civilian, was affecting him nonetheless.

When Barber told me what had happened on the bridge, my hackles rose. We were sitting alone in the wardroom. I wanted to say, "Why don't you and Tourneau fight?" as if I needed combat, if only vicariously.

"What are you going to do about it?" I asked loudly.

"I don't know yet."

"You're being screwed," I almost shouted with all my resonance.

"I know," said Barber with a distant look, as if he was absently studying a berg on the far horizon.

Observing his Adam's apple, I felt increasingly jumpy. Yet I found it a very interesting conflict, a means of whiling away some icebreaker boredom. The boredom too was very interesting. If I hadn't experienced it I would have thought it incredible. A wild sea. Gorgeous ice pieces. Exotic birds. Extreme geographic remoteness. And boredom. I considered, with apologies to Adelie penguins, of whom I was fond, the possibility that maybe it was Hank Elkins, not the birders, with the birdbrain.

* * *

It was early afternoon of the same day. Barber and I, sitting at the wardroom dining table, were having coffee. The fiddle had been removed, as it always was between meals. I was reading the proceedings of a conference about the importance of Antarctica as the new frontier in international law. Barber was making notations in a journal book. Engine noises, and a general, usual rattling of things. Standing up, he took his cup to the galley for a refill, handing it to the young messman dressed in whites. The small galley, separated from the main room by two swinging half-doors and a wooden, hip-high shelf, was at the aft, starboard end of the room.

The messman filled Barber's cup, leaned forward with a frown and asked tensely in a husky whisper, "Mr. Barber. Sir, may I speak to you about something?"

He was tall, blond, very thin, and had a long, thin neck. Recalling that he had officer status on the ship and that at times on the weather decks crewmen with throwaway or point-and-shoot cameras would come up to him respectfully to ask about the cameras he was using, Barber replied, "Sure. What's your name?"

"Yost. Kenny Yost, sir." Staring at him, the messman said, "Mr. Barber, the CO puts the ship above the crew. The CO don't give a shit about the crew. There were times when we were on water hours. Fresh water was restricted. We were restricted taking showers, doing laundry, flushing. We practically couldn't brush our fucking teeth. Yet he ordered us to scrub down some of the decks with fresh water. That message means you're shit, so eat shit. Mr. Barber, can you please help us?"

Barber felt a surge of empathy. Yost's long, thin neck made him seem very vulnerable.

"Why tell *me* about it?" he asked.

"Because you have influence."

"I probably can't even help myself," Barber thought.

"I'd like to help you," he said, "but I'm only a civilian guest. Sorry."

Returning to his seat, he told me quietly what the messman had said. I glanced around the room. Men chatting, reading, writing. Nobody but me seemed to know about the exchange.

I said, "Remember Harry Easton's telling us about Tourneau's making ugly public comments at McMurdo? And refusing to manifest you because of what, in his opinion, were unclear orders written by Easton? And calling you a freeloader? What does this dude gain by alienating you? He's making an interesting mistake in taking on a civilian as well as military people—people who are little people, in his opinion. He no doubt brown-noses those above him. George, are you little people?"

Although Barber's smile was usually shy though warm, he could burst into surprisingly exuberant, open, generous, infectious laughter, when all of him seemed to let go. He laughed like that now and my recent, growing hostility seemed to abate.

"I've heard, but only in general, about your D.C. connections," I said. "Word gets around. Larry Minsky, one of the helo pilots, said you must have White House pull, because you're the only one in Antarctica not working. I noticed that Easton handled you with kid gloves. Tell me about your D.C. connections, George."

Barber laughed again and resumed jotting in his notebook.

"You feel flattered because the messman, and presumably other enlisted men, singled you out to ask for help?" I asked.

"I'd like to help. I'm embarrassed because I can't."

"Not even with your D.C. influence?"

Smiling shyly, Barber shrugged. I wondered what that influence could be. Was it real or dreamed up? And why was Barber playing his cards so close to his chest? If he had real D.C. influence

(I couldn't imagine what it might be) why didn't he speak up, make it felt, clobber somebody, preferably Tourneau?

* * *

About an hour later, a little before dinner, while Barber and I were chatting in the wardroom, the executive officer (XO), a commander named Al Carpenter, tall, large, handsome, with an engaging, open face and manner, approached, bent over Barber and whispered, "Mr. Barber, may I meet with you in my office after dinner?"

"Okay," said Barber.

"I'll come and fetch you."

And so Carpenter did, leading Barber not through the wardroom's main, aft door but through the forward one alongside the galley, which he and Tourneau normally used and which Barber and I occasionally used late at night, especially after poker, to descend to the enlisted men's mess for midrats (midnight rations, like macaroni with soft boysenberry ice cream), served cafeteria style. The ship was rolling heavily as Barber followed Carpenter to the latter's office two flights below the wardroom deck. Wondering what Carpenter wanted to speak with him about, Barber used the steel stairs with caution, impressed with the ease and grace, almost like those of a professional ballroom dancer or figure skater, with which Carpenter, though somewhat overweight, was handling them.

In his office Carpenter shut the door, turned to Barber and said sharply, "Mr. Barber, the CO is incensed because you conducted an interview with Messman Yost! We know what Yost told you—about the ship being on short water rations, yet the CO had the decks washed down with fresh water to make a good impression on two visitors, and about the CO's not caring about his crew. Yost isn't qualified to have expert opinions about this ship. The CO requires that no interviews be held without his permission. And we know you took pictures belowdecks and photographed the broken winch. The captain forbids you to take pictures belowdecks without his permission. Is that clear? We could confiscate your films."

Barber was surprised and stunned by the heat and content of this outburst. He recalled that Jack Tourneau, in dealing with Easton, had resisted manifesting him, Barber, on the ship; that Jack Tourneau had called him a freeloader while speaking with Easton; that he, Barber, had been assigned a CPOQ rack; that Tourneau still avoided eye contact with him; that Sonny Peterson had insulted him by suggesting he secretly carried a tape recorder; and above all that he was being deprived of the liberty of the bridge.

"Mr. Carpenter, I invite you to confiscate them," he said softly. "You're stronger than I, there are more *of* you, so I can't stop you. But if you do, my lawyers will investigate whether the Coast Guard has the right to confiscate the private property of an American civilian on the high seas. I was never forbidden to take photos belowdecks. And I didn't shoot the broken winch, so your informant or informants are mistaken or lying. I shot only Chief Flynn and the phone shack. Hank Elkins is a witness. Anyhow, why would I want to shoot the winch? My film is totally my property. I'm here on my own resources. I'm not a grantee on a per diem."

"You're lucky this is happening in Antarctica, where there's no law covering civilians, otherwise a Federal court would force you to hand them over."

"I have sufficient confidence in our laws to believe they're designed to protect *all* of us, including me and my private property. How would you like it if I asked the Federal courts or a powerful member of Congress to protect me from the Coast Guard?"

"Well, we *won't* confiscate them," said Carpenter angrily, bouncing up and down on the balls of his feet as if he was in *The Sleeping Beauty*, causing Barber to wonder if he had studied ballet as a boy.

"What am I doing in this office," Barber thought, "with its super-neatness, super-coziness, its photographic reminders of this man's wife and kids? The bridge is where I should be."

He resolved that Tourneau and Carpenter would learn they had made a serious mistake in coming to open grips with him. What they didn't realize was that in some ways he enjoyed this kind of confrontation and therefore thrived on it and that he rarely played this kind of game unless he was sure he held a winning hand.

"Who told Tourneau about Yost's talk with me and about my photographing belowdecks?" he asked icily.

It was a dramatic change of tone, and his gaze had turned confrontational.

"I can't reveal that."

"Mr. Carpenter, you're beyond your depth. As for your being only a go-between, that remains to be seen. So Tourneau has a grievance? I have one too—no access to the bridge, a restriction that deprives me of the ability to perform my official duties. So Tourneau is incensed? Tourneau and you too, Mr. Carpenter, may wish to consider the degree to which *I'm* incensed—about being spied upon as an official civilian guest on an American military ship. It's Tourneau who's behaving improperly—by slighting me, by depriving me of access to the Southern Ocean and parts of this ship, by making false accusations against me and by having me spied on.

"You and Tourneau are misinformed. I didn't approach Yost or any other crewman. I neither requested nor conducted an interview. Yost asked if he could speak with me. I said okay. I had no idea what he wanted to talk about. We had never talked before. I'm obviously not in a position to judge the merits of his complaints but if I learn that he's punished for speaking to me, I'll make it my business to mention the matter to some of my influential friends.

"It's Tourneau's duty in the chain of command to provide me with transportation from McMurdo to Palmer Station and to afford me the unobstructed opportunity to do my work. I remind you and Tourneau that the PENGUIN is part of a Navy task force the prime function of which, south of Sixty Degrees South latitude, is to supply logistic support for scientists and other personnel working under grants and the general supervision of the National Endowment for Science, and that this structure stems from the White House itself under the authorization of Congress.

"It will make an interesting story back home if it becomes widely known that I was unwelcome on the bridge of an American ship despite express orders that the bridge be made available to me."

"We're aware of your Senatorial connections," said Carpenter almost in a whisper, again bouncing as if he was doing entrechats.

"Ah," thought Barber, "so that's your game. Right, then we'll have a show of power," and he imagined a call being made on a certain Senator's behalf to Coast Guard headquarters in Washington or even to the Department of Transportation, which had jurisdiction over the Coast Guard in peacetime, and how quite suddenly Tourneau would become a Coast Guard embarrassment, a Coast Guard burden.

"Senatorial connections?" he said. "Mr. Carpenter, in that case you're an even less prudent man than I thought. Until your remark I considered that you were merely Tourneau's messenger, as you implied you were. I now believe that both you and Tourneau are obstructing me in the performance of my duties under the chain of command, and I'll be glad to make a call to Washington to help straighten you both out. I have good reason to believe that Coast Guard headquarters will take a special interest in this case, and will divorce themselves from your and Tourneau's obstructionist behavior."

Looking alarmed, and bending his dancer's knees to lower his height, Carpenter said urgently, "Mr. Barber, I don't want to be caught in a crossfire. I'm only relaying a message from the CO. I'll be happy to convey your bridge grievance to him."

"The sooner the better," said Barber.

Hoping to mollify Barber, Carpenter gently touched his arm as they left his quarters and returned to the wardroom, where he was unusually attentive to Barber and gave the impression of being on friendly terms with him. Barber found it hard to unbend. The effects of isolation and severe weather which were part of Southern Ocean life were affecting everyone. A part of Barber hoped Tourneau would sense the weakness of his own position and the kind of opponent Barber could be. Barber had no wish to have the hard, perhaps ugly, side of himself surface during this fascinating voyage.

* * *

Alone with me in the wardroom, Barber told me about his meeting with Carpenter. I was surprised and pleased he had defended himself aggressively. Like him, I was amazed that he and Yost had been spied on. We speculated how that might have been accomplished, not failing to see a certain humor inherent in the situation.

Who could have overheard the exchange between Barber and Yost? And who had reported it so promptly to Tourneau? Of the several people who had been in the wardroom, we were familiar with two, Ollie Buxtehude (one of the birders) and Ben Paduani. But though we had no love lost for Buxtehude, an arrogant native Californian, we couldn't imagine why a civilian would want to involve himself in such a business, unless the endless binocular birding had softened his bird-brain. As for Paduani, we somehow doubted that he needed to show military solidarity with Tourneau by snitching for him.

Barber's back had been turned toward the wardroom, so he had been unable to see who was listening in on the so-called interview, and he had been absorbed in listening to Yost's complaints. Why hadn't Yost noticed that someone in the wardroom was tuning in? Had Barber's body cut off his view of the room? Yost had almost whispered, and we had been pitching and rolling, and creaking loudly. Not to forget the ever-present background of engine noises. So we couldn't see how anybody could have overheard the exchange. Even if the room had contained an expert lip-reader, how could the latter have been able to see Yost's mouth past Barber's body?

Was the galley bugged? Had there been a second messman in it, whom Barber hadn't noticed? Had Yost been overheard telling about his meeting with Barber, and had a crewman betrayed him? Then the most far-out question of all: was Yost part of an entrapment scheme? And who had reported Barber's taking photos of Flynn and the phone shack? Flynn? It seemed unlikely. And why was Tourneau worrying about the winch's being photographed? What did the winch's failure mean?

What kind of dude was this CO, who cared so little about his PR? What was he after and where was he heading? We wondered about the appropriateness of his being in the military. How had such a psychic structure managed to survive moving up in the ranks? Wouldn't he have been happier as a vice president for public affairs in some large industrial company, say one specializing in making exotic fragrances? My brother-in-law, Andy Fox, an executive in such a company, had given me some details. For example, the aroma of a flower on a living plant is molecularly different from the aroma of the same flower if the flower has been cut off from the plant, and the difference is detectable almost immediately. The reason: biological death in the cut flower occurs rapidly, showing up molecularly in its aroma. It seems that death likes to advertise its presence.

Until recently certain flowers (orchids, say) couldn't be made into perfume because they didn't produce oil, but with the latest technology (tiny air pumps, tiny air traps, spectroscopy, computers, miniature robots) oil could be bypassed and the aroma molecules analyzed and identified, then synthesized to produce new (and expensive) fragrances. The best and most expensive attar of roses came from Bulgaria. Andy showed me a modest container, about two quarts, of Bulgarian rose oil that cost twenty-five or thirty thousand dollars and had the distinction of being kept in a room whose walls were a ten-foot-high chain-link fence. This was in a building that reminded me of a large airplane hangar.

Peter Markovsky joined us at the wardroom table and I told him about Carpenter's threat to confiscate Barber's films. I shared this information with him because, knowing Peter to be something of an expert on international law, I wanted his reaction.

"What do you think?" I asked.

"Well, international law with respect to the Antarctic is quite strange," he said in his foreign accent, lighting his pipe with his Cartier gold lighter. "For example, consider the Ross Ice Shelf, which is approximately the size of France. It's afloat, and attached to land only by being aground in certain places. It's neither land nor sea, so it falls under neither the Law of the Land nor the Law of the Sea. So what do you do if a civilian of Nation A murders a civilian of Nation A on it? Or if a civilian of Nation A murders a civilian of Nation B on it? Under what law and in what jurisdiction would you prosecute? A military person of Nation A murdering a military person or a civilian of Nation A on it would present less of a problem, because such a case would usually fall under military law. But what if a military person of Nation A murders a military person of Nation B on it? Or if a civilian of Nation A murders a military person of Nation A on it? Or if a civilian of Nation A murders a military person of Nation B on it? And consider that inasmuch as part of the Southern Ocean—everything south of Sixty Degrees South—is included in the Antarctic Treaty, that part is in some respects treated as if it's part of Antarctica. Complex enough for you?"

FIVE

Hoping for a phone call to the States, Barber and I went down to the phone shack. Somewhere, I wasn't sure on which deck, we saw Yost at a distance. He seemed to be signaling to us. At first I took it to be Churchill's V sign, until it reminded me of the Boy Scout sign: three fingers of the right hand upraised, right thumb resting on the right pinky nail. As we made a move to approach him he disappeared.

The queue at the shack was very long, so we headed for the wardroom. Again we spotted Yost. The messman, flushing, joined us. He looked like a sensitive, decent young guy.

"Mr. Barber, I've been threatened with sick bay if I talk to you again," he said.

"Sick bay?" I asked.

"We have no brig. A brig is in a remote place. You have to waste manpower, have somebody guard the prisoner so he can be freed in case of an emergency. So sick bay is used as the brig."

"Who reported your speaking with Mr. Barber?" I asked.

"Don't know."

"You mention it to anybody?"

"No sir. Sir, the captain has spies."

"Know that for a fact?" I asked.

"It's what the guys say. There's hard feelings against the captain among the crew. He better not walk alone on deck the way he usually does."

"Don't talk like that," I said.

"Why not?"

"If anything happens you may be a prime suspect," said Barber.

"I'd be one anyway."

I thought, "Can this nice-looking, sad-looking kid with the long, lever-like legs, caught in a military web, be capable of murder?"

"Mr. Barber, I'm just a New Hampshire boy," said Yost. "*Live Free Or Die* says our state license plate. I was raised with women—

three sisters and my mom, all with the same initial—Betty, Bonnie, Bea, Brigid. My dad died long ago. They mothered me half to death. I'd get to breaking things. Once, I slashed a couch pillow. It made them cry. My mom walloped me. She was bugging me. Some chores I hadn't done. It was winter. The chores were in the dark, outside. I was scared of the dark. Mr. Barber, can you please help us?"

"Mr. Barber has no power on this ship," I said.

"It's not what the scuttlebutt says."

"Take care of yourself," said Barber, frowning as we parted.

A couple of hours later we were hanging out in the wardroom as usual and I went to the door of the pantry for a coffee refill. The young messman on duty, stout in contrast with Yost, leaning toward me, whispered, "Mr. Elkins, Kenny's in sick bay."

"Say what?"

"In sick bay."

"Punished for talking to Mr. Barber?"

"You got it."

Rejoining Barber at the table, I informed him in a whisper. He responded with only a scowl. Nor did he refer to this episode again, disappointing me and again causing me to wonder if he had a cowardly streak.

* * *

What with the irritating noises of ship and sea, and the pitching, rolling and yawing that had thoroughly gotten to me, it wasn't easy to play detective. Anyhow, who would normally care about these drama tidbits? I had long ago been hardened to such stuff in the bureaucratic world I inhabited. But the fact was, I had been sucked into the maw of the icebreaker's effervescences and by now lacked the will to free myself. I was ripe for a sea soap opera that promised to be a Large Event.

Where was sick bay? Would Barber and I be allowed to visit Yost there? How could it happen that once again Barber and Yost had been overheard? I could swear there was no visible witness to Barber's and my meeting with Yost. But I couldn't take an oath that I had carefully checked our surroundings for possible spies. I expected Barber to pose questions. Yost? Sick bay? Spies? If he did, he failed to share them with me, and inasmuch as I considered Yost to be essentially *his* problem I accepted his silence. What with Leelee in my life and the growing possibility of a divorce, I had enough to cope with. My current job was Antarctic Observer, not Southern Ocean Activist.

* * *

About twenty-four hours after Barber's private meeting with Carpenter, Carpenter approached him, again in the wardroom after dinner, and whispered, "The CO wishes to speak with you in his cabin."

Upon which Barber followed Carpenter from the wardroom to Tourneau's quarters two decks below.

Smiling self-confidently, Tourneau greeted Barber at the door of his cabin with a nod, glanced at Carpenter, who was sitting down on a couch, and said, "Please be seated. I understand you have a problem," taking a seat on a captain's chair.

This was their first meeting, and Tourneau was no longer avoiding direct eye contact with Barber. Barber, sensing Tourneau had been thoroughly briefed about his meeting with Carpenter, was aware of the spacious, elegant and brightly illuminated cabin, which he compared with the darkness of CPOQ.

"Indeed I have a problem," he said, studying Tourneau.

Curly reddish hair verging on sandy. Reddish mustache trimmed with great care, the edge looking sharp enough to cut a finger. Blue right eye turned slightly inward, a condition Barber assumed went back to Tourneau's childhood. The poor posture Barber recalled from the nightly movies. Small feet crossed. Sensitive hands lying loosely on the arms of the oak chair. The massive Burmese ruby ring, adorning the left pinky, occasionally flashing a deep cherry light.

"I'm being denied access to the bridge when the weather decks are secured," said Barber. "I'm deprived of the ability to perform my duties, which are to observe the PENGUIN and the Southern Ocean in all weather."

"My instructions don't include your working on my ship," said Tourneau stiffly, torso leaning forward. "They specify only that I'm to transport you from McMurdo to Palmer."

"I haven't seen them, but if that's the case, you've been misinformed. A message to Easton at McMurdo will quickly clarify the situation."

"I have no intention of communicating with Easton," said Tourneau crisply. "My superior is not Easton, but Captain Swinburne, the Navy task force commander. My instructions regarding you are absolutely clear. I don't need to communicate with anybody about them."

"In that case I'm prepared to do some communicating myself. Let me speak plainly. I didn't ask to speak to Yost. I didn't interview Yost. I asked him no questions. I merely listened to his complaints. I've violated no rules of this ship. I trust Mr. Carpenter has made that clear. I object to your leaping to the conclusion that I interviewed Yost. You could have asked me if I interviewed him."

"I have my own opinion as to what really happened, and I stand by it."

"Would you care to produce a witness? I'll be glad to question him in your presence."

"I would *not*. This is *my* ship, and *I* decide how it's run."

"By disobeying orders in denying me the use of the bridge? What function does a snitcher have in this case? Who told you I took photos belowdecks? And misinformed you by reporting I shot the broken winch? Is this a Big Brother ship you're running?"

"Mr. Barber, you're impertinent!" said Carpenter angrily.

"And you? And Mr. Tourneau? You aren't impertinent in falsely accusing me?"

"You're a freeloader," said Tourneau contemptuously. "What's the country getting out of your being here?"

Barber remembered Paduani asking the identical question.

"May I quote you?" he asked.

"You may *not*. You may not quote anything I've said. But you will."

"I see you think you can predict my behavior."

"I'll stand by my present orders. I'm responsible for the safety of this ship and its personnel. Allowing you on the bridge would be a present danger to ship and crew."

"How? The bridge is spacious. What could I do? Grab some instrument I don't understand?"

"I'll stand by what I just said."

"I'll be glad to work on either of the bridge wings even though they're unprotected against the weather. Would you consider me a threat to the ship's safety on the wings?"

"Absolutely. I have no orders that include your working on my ship. Until I receive such orders, I stand by my present ones."

"Mr. Tourneau, I don't in the least confuse your strange, unfriendly behavior toward me with the great institution you serve. Time is of the essence for my project. I doubt I'll ever have a chance to repeat this voyage. I'm possibly losing precious opportunities by the hour. I advise you to be realistic, because if necessary I'll do my duty and let the public know what kind of reception I received on your ship, including if necessary bringing your behavior to the attention of a powerful Senator."

"That sounds like a threat."

"It's a promise."

"We know about your Senatorial connections. All it proves is the power of Congress."

"The power of Congress, and the structure of our democracy, are good enough for me. I have ways of either changing your orders or your interpretation of them. I give you two choices. I can call the Senator and report that you're deliberately obstructing me in the performance of my duties. I have good reason to believe he'll have a call made to Coast Guard headquarters about you, and headquarters will spin you around in mid-ocean."

"That's going pretty far," said Tourneau, turning pale.

"I agree. The second choice is, I'll radio Harry Easton myself and ask him to clarify your orders, if necessary by informing Captain Swinburne of your obstruction of my work."

"I'll give your message the highest priority," Tourneau said with a grin suggesting he expected Barber's request to be ignored or denied.

"I'll write the message immediately," said Barber and left the cabin.

He went to his locker, reached for a pad and pencil and, in the dim reddish light emanating from the bulb above the head's door, stopped to consider. He recalled Harry Easton's tight little mouth back in McMurdo. It was a remarkable mouth, it deserved a good photo. Barber couldn't recall seeing another as determined to suggest a hyphen. What did the mouth mean? Was its chief task to contain the rep's explosive anger?

It was in his, Barber's, favor that Harry Easton disliked Tourneau, judging by what the former had said about the latter in the Chalet, but would that play a significant role in Easton's bureaucratic decision? Barber sensed that Easton was a guy who would lean over backward to be fair. Of two things Barber was certain: the correctness of his behavior on the PENGUIN and that he held strong cards. He was reasonably sure of his ground and about how stubborn and persistent he could be if forced against the wall.

Bridling, he recalled Tourneau's calling him a freeloader. Where had the son of a bitch picked up such a notion? Although Barber would have preferred not to fight, he told himself that if humiliation was Tourneau's game, Tourneau had made a serious mistake.

Should he address himself to the Navy task force commander, whom he knew only slightly? Or should he stay within the chain of command by going to Easton? Would Easton really back him up? Easton had backed down and rewritten Barber's travel orders when Tourneau had complained they were too vague. Was Easton capable of standing up to Captain Swinburne if the latter supported Tourneau? How D.C. savvy were Easton and Swinburne? Would Tourneau really send Barber's message? Would he give Barber the reply if there was one? Would he abide by it if it countermanded him? It was the task force's primary function to support the National Endowment for Science in Antarctica. Therefore Easton, as the NES Antarctic rep, had some real power, provided he was willing to use it.

Barber resolved that if he didn't receive prompt support from Easton, he would show both Easton and Tourneau just how powerful a senior Senator could be, and how insignificant they were in the D.C. scheme of things. Barber was prepared, in short, to educate them, Tourneau in particular, in the political realities.

Warmed by the memory of the flap Tourneau had created at McMurdo, irritating Easton and possibly Swinburne as well, Barber, bracing himself as the ship rolled heavily, scrawled a message, which he checked by the head's dazzling light.

FROM USCGC PENGUIN TO HARRY EASTON MCMURDO
ANTARCTICA. PLEASE BE ADVISED I DO NOT HAVE AC-
CESS TO THE BRIDGE AND THAT SUCH ACCESS WHEN
LOWER DECKS ARE SECURED WOULD BE MOST HELPFUL
TO MY GATHERING MATERIALS RE PENGUIN AND SOUTH-
ERN OCEAN FOR MY BOOK. GEORGE BARBER.

He went to the wardroom and handed the message to Carpenter,
who disappeared with it and soon returned, giving Barber a copy of
the transmitted version. All this occurred before the evening movie.
When Barber told me about these developments, I asked, "How did
the XO and CO learn about your 'Senatorial connections'?"

"I don't know. Think Easton will ignore me?"

"It would be dangerous for him. He's no doubt heard about your
Senatorial connections."

* * *

Inasmuch as Tourneau had been publicly ignoring Barber, Barber
made no effort to keep his problems with the CO private, and I myself saw no reason to protect Tourneau's reputation when he himself
was so lax about it. So word about their conflict, including Barber's
"interview" with Yost, spread in the wardroom.

"The pilots, to a man, are rooting for Barber," Roger Dove, the
senior helo pilot, said to me. He had a gentle, smiling, generous,
brown-bearded face.

The helo pilots were now openly friendly to Barber in Tourneau's
presence at the movies, a fact Tourneau pretended not to notice.

"It may simply be a technical matter," said Markovsky. "If the
CO's orders are unclear, Easton will need to clarify them. But the
CO has ignored the political realities. Not surprising in certain mil-
itary types. He's opened a can of worms."

* * *

We were taking rolls of forty and forty-five degrees. They were eas-
iest for Barber to handle lying down. If he stood they took his breath
away after centrifuging his gut, then suddenly reversed direction. He

learned to walk while leaning like the Tower of Pisa. When he sat, the wired-down chairs and his body had unpleasant confrontations, and parts of him ached afterwards. Occasionally he tried sitting on a corner of the wardroom aft couch, near the little projection booth, where guests' parkas were piled. He'd soon find himself falling on his side. His leg muscles and lower back would ache from trying to keep him upright, so he'd switch to a chair.

Some of us, myself included, now slept through mealtime or were too sick to eat. I never threw up but nor was I okay. Barber was among those who stayed well, maybe because he was so physically fit, but more likely because he was dedicated to his work, driven to *see* with those intense brown eyes as though he was their slave, and to try to share what he saw.

Now and then the icebreaker would start keeling over and keep going beyond the point where Barber expected it to stop. Then it would go still further, until he'd think, "Okay, enough!" But it wasn't, and he'd wonder when it *would* stop, and he'd hold his breath and think, "Now it *must* stop!" Yet the roll would continue until the ship seemed about to lie on its side, and he'd think, "This is now *dangerous!*" The ship would pause, hover, tremble, then at last change roll direction, and his organs and muscles would scramble to make the necessary adjustments.

Later, when we resumed our normal rolls, he'd wonder just how large a particular roll had been. A couple of times, phoning the bridge from the wardroom, he learned that what he had assumed was a fifty-degree roll was just a forty or forty-two, but coming suddenly after a series of twenties and twenty-fives, its effect had been extraordinary.

He found himself wishing the ship would settle down for just a little while so he could remember what life was like when the world was stable underfoot. With such rolling and pitching it wasn't possible to walk steadily. He could hardly call it walking, nor could he call it dancing. It was a wild weaving, in which he tried not to slam into things. Once, while stretching to touch his toes, he almost fell on his face because of a sudden heavy roll. In the head that morning, while brushing his teeth, he had been flung into the shower stall and been surprised he wasn't hurt.

* * *

Time was passing in slow motion. The weather had slowed down his time sense and retarded his metabolism. With nothing interesting happening *out there*, he tended to feel that nothing interesting was happening anywhere. The need for Large Events sometimes took us both to the ship's store. We had shopped in the Navy PX in Christchurch and at McMurdo, but the same items when viewed in the PENGUIN's PX looked magical because they were displaced in some mysterious and profound way. We got very tired doing nothing. We throve on Events, however inconsequential. Film, sheath knives and shaving cream in a PX located below waterline created a world apart, remote from the unpleasantness of the Southern Ocean.

* * *

Occasionally Barber thought he'd just sit in the wardroom and meditate a while, but the brief sits sometimes lasted an hour or more, during which he slept as if drugged. It took determination and concentration to do more than sit like that. Just to stand up required a surprising amount of will power. To walk was a feat, because it meant dealing with decks that in McMurdo Sound and the southern reaches of the Ross Sea had been friendly but which now either pressed aggressively against the soles of his boots or gave him the impression of suddenly abandoning him, like a quickly descending elevator. He did things begrudgingly, in slow motion and in a mental fog.

The icebreaker's gyrations sometimes made him despise his consciousness, which was partly why he slept. He didn't despise the Southern Ocean. The Southern Ocean was Nature. It was he who was at fault. He forgot that he was Nature too. When he handled the ship and the Southern Ocean well, his self-confidence made a quantum leap forward, as if he was a kind of hero.

There were times when he was particularly irritated by the ship's gyrations, as if they meant to spite him personally. The ship would fall down one ocean hill and be hurled sideways by another while still descending. At times it pitched and rolled simultaneously, or stood on its stern, the bow lifted so high it obscured the horizon. The bow seemed to quiver. Down it came, crashing, and white water flew, spray drenching the fo'c'sle, which took spouts of white water through the scuppers. The sea's gray turned to whorls of purple near the prow.

When he had to take a leak it was a challenge to reach the head without falling or being slammed against metal. The urinal heaved. He had to wait patiently for his urinary sphincter to relax. His breath often came in short rhythms. Sometimes he shut his eyes in an effort to endure the discomfort but it wasn't always safe to do so. Things fought him: a heavy metal door, a steep-pitched metal stairway, his rack, the deck. At times his brain felt as if it was splashing around in his skull. He was really comfortable only when he slept, but even then he was sometimes awakened by the ship's heaviest rolls.

Compounding everything was the fact that he felt trapped. But the ship he felt trapped in was also preserving him. When he felt the ship falling down a mountainous swell as if on a roller coaster and felt his gut falling with it he was thankful to be trapped.

* * *

During lunch some forty hours after Barber sent the message to Easton, Al Carpenter entered the wardroom, approached Barber, bent down and whispered, "Your request has been granted. You may use the bridge when the weather decks are secured."

"Thank you," said Barber with a little nod, feeling relieved.

But when, about an hour later, he read Easton's message in the message traffic book hung on a wardroom wall near the pantry, he got an even more pleasant surprise, for Easton had on his own initiative broadened his request.

TO USCGC PENGUIN. MR BARBER INTERESTED IN ALL ASPECTS OF US ANTARCTIC PROGRAM INCLUDING VITAL ROLE OF US COAST GUARD. REQUEST YOU ALLOW MR BARBER ACCESS TO VARIOUS PARTS OF PENGUIN DURING ALL WEATHER. EASTON.

Barber asked Carpenter, who was in the wardroom, for a copy of Easton's reply, which the XO promptly fetched. The message's effect on Carpenter was marked. He took every opportunity short of

actual statements to let Barber sense his neutrality in the trouble between Tourneau and Barber. Barber noticed that Peterson, the fat-
assed operations officer who had ordered him off the bridge, was
now wary of him and stayed out of his way.

"I have no wish to exploit Easton's message," Barber told me.
"I'll use the bridge as infrequently as possible, and only when the
weather decks are secured."

There was some speculation in the wardroom about how
Tourneau would react to the message. Would he ignore it? Would he
stall, using up Barber's ship time?

"It's outrageous for a civilian to call the shots on a Coast Guard
ship," Paduani said angrily to Barber. "You'll soon leave the ship
and put the experience behind you. But the CO's loss of face with
the crew will haunt him. You can bet Easton sent copies of his message to Washington."

"The CO had it coming," I said. "He *knew* about George's 'Senatorial connections.' Easton obeyed a good bureaucrat's first com-
mandment—cover your ass."

Barber, as I expected, said nothing.

* * *

The only direct light was an intriguing, fierce white band made by a
seemingly tiny berg on the far horizon. The almost muscular light was
a relief from the visual monotony of sky and water, water and sky, day
after day. High, lurching green waves with whitecaps. Our hull slapping the water as we rolled. An Antarctic petrel skimming the waves
and dipping a wing off our starboard. White breast and underwings,
black head and tail. The air tasting good deep in my lungs.

SIX

It was after dinner, and Barber and I were waiting in line for a phone call in the bowels of the ship, when Chief Flynn, once again the phone operator, got a call and surprised Barber by handing him the phone, saying, "XO."

"Mr. Barber," said Al Carpenter, "we've been looking all over for you. I sent somebody to check if you were in your rack. Somebody else was despatched to the weather decks. We wondered where you had disappeared to, until a crewman reported seeing you in the phone shack's vicinity. The CO would like you to report to the bridge. He said the seas are the kind you're interested in. Will you come?"

"Yes."

When Barber gave me the gist of the call, I said, "So they were searching for you all over the fucking ship! The CO's covering his ass."

Barber had an impulse to hurry to the bridge, partly to make peace with Tourneau. But then he considered the lateness of the hour, the loss of daylight, the slowness of his preferred color film in the Antarctic (Kodachrome 25), and his belief that he took the best pictures when responding to his own inspiration, not someone else's. Also, he was irritated by what he felt was an invasion of his privacy. Still, wanting to avoid even the appearance of further conflict, he fetched two cameras from his locker and proceeded to the bridge. Jack Tourneau wasn't there. The bridge that had seemed exotic when forbidden was now prosaic, as it had once been. Barber would have been pleased to see Sonny Peterson, with his vacuous face and seam-threatening butt, so he could lord it over him a bit, but Peterson too was absent. As Barber had expected, the light outside was too dim. The two birders were staring at a gloomy, gray veil of weather. Replacing the cameras in his locker, Barber went to the wardroom.

Next day he and I were on the fantail when the PA boomed, "Mr. Barber's presence is requested on the bridge!"

"I can't believe this dude," I said. "Apologizing publicly!"

Again Barber felt his privacy was being invaded. But, eager to keep the peace, and not wanting to miss a possibly promising shoot, he went to the bridge. Tourneau, Pentax in hand, and wearing a khaki cap, khaki trousers and a dark windbreaker, was standing on the starboard bridge wing.

"I thought you'd like to see twin bergs we're approaching," he said, looking directly at Barber and smiling and sounding friendly. "Sea soundings show a couple of thousand feet. I'm not sure they're joined below the surface but I expect we'll pass between them."

"Thanks for the call," said Barber, joining him on the wing.

"No problem."

The bergs were several miles away. One, massive, was tabular. The other, showing an upthrust arm with torch, supported by ample folds of clothing, reminded Barber of the Statue of Liberty. As the ship drew close, he saw that the bergs rested on a marble-like pedestal carved smooth by waves. The PA announced the bergs' presence, and crewmen appeared on the weather decks, some with cameras. The ship moved between the two berg sections.

"We're getting a sounding of only a hundred feet, so it's clear they're joined," remarked Tourneau.

"What if the berg suddenly heaves?" wondered Barber while shooting. "He must know Antarctic sea ice is notoriously unpredictable."

The tabular berg loomed. Its massive sides, resembling an earth cliff, showed annual striations and a texture resembling a cross-section of bone. Lavender-tinted water restlessly reflected the twin bergs' lights and shadows.

As the ship slid between the bergs, the contrast between the smooth ivory pedestal and several roughly carved upper shapes reminded Barber of deliberately unfinished statues by Michelangelo. Electric blues and greens against a pearl-gray sky.

"What if the strait suddenly turns shallow?" I said to Peter Markovsky, who was standing beside me in the bow. "Why is the

CO walking a tightrope? Why is he publicly sucking up to George? It's obscene."

We slid between the bergs without incident. Glancing back, I saw them being obscured by brown smoke belching from our stack.

Later, Roger Dove remarked privately to Barber and me, "What stupid thing will the CO do next? I and the other pilots, especially Minsky, have an uneasy feeling about him." Turning to Barber with a smile, he said drily, "I see you've got him on the run."

"I overheard Minsky say he wouldn't mind if the CO falls overboard in foul weather," I said. "Made me wonder if he meant foul play."

Dove laughed. "I suspect some of the enlisted men, though, wouldn't mind if the CO got lost," he said.

* * *

Early next day we approached at close range a berg of legendary proportions, which had been first sighted by satellite. It was sixty-five by eighty miles, larger than Connecticut, and was estimated to weigh about three hundred billion tons. The ice shelf of which it had been a part stood almost two hundred feet above sea level, was thirteen hundred feet thick and floated on three thousand feet of water. This berg was so large it made its own weather. Being colder than the water supporting it, it created great quantities of mist and fog. It posed a threat to ships, for it wasn't yet on any map and was in constant though slow northward motion. "The mother of all fucking bergs," somebody said.

"It's like God," someone else said.

Instead of taking care to avoid it, Tourneau set our course just to the north of it. From a distance it suggested a great, fuzzy fog bank hugging the horizon. A stretch of water so blue it verged on violet. Spectral light in a herringbone sky. Water turning obsidian. Our wake like curdled milk. A Mincke whale breaching off our starboard a quarter of a mile away. The berg's outlines remained uncertain until we were close to it. The water in its vicinity was littered with small ice fragments about the size of growlers.

"The CO may be endangering the ship by getting so close," said Dove to Barber and me in the bow. "You can never know when parts of a huge berg may calve off."

Again nothing untoward happened.

During lunch Al Carpenter approached Barber, bent over and whispered, "The CO invites you and the Observation Team to dinner in his cabin this evening at 1730. Accept?"

"Yes."

Carpenter looked relieved.

* * *

And so there was Barber at the head of the captain's table, at Tourneau's request. Tourneau at Barber's left. I, also at Tourneau's request, at the foot. Jack Tourneau eyeing Barber often and steadily, almost staring at him. So much for refusing to have eye contact with him. George Barber being as taciturn as tall, gaunt, round-shouldered Edward Hopper, the great American painter. His Picasso eyes were now seemingly hooded, as if searching inward. I could no more read him than I could Tourneau.

White-gloved, dark-skinned steward. White-clad chef. White linen. Candles. Silk flowers (white roses, red peonies, mums, violets, sprays of fern) swelling from a shiny brass urn. Goblets of icewater. Glasses of chilled sauterne beaded with condensation. Shrimp cocktail with fresh lemon. Marsala chicken with spinach and mashed potatoes. Cherry sauce over vanilla ice cream.

"Mr. Barber," said Tourneau, lifting his glass of water with a broad, friendly smile and shaking it to make the ice cubes tinkle, "you think this is ordinary ice. Correct?"

He was wearing a pinky ring on his left hand. Paduani later told me it was an eight-carat natural citrine, pale lime in color, quite rare, set in 18K yellow gold and made by Cartier in London. This studly dude with delicate hands liked to wear rings more appropriate for a woman. Did he have other rings on board? A jewelry case groaning with them? I would have loved to examine it. And to view his psychic structure, with its varied inclusions. I knew something about jewelry. My association with Leelee and her family had inevitably taught me a few things about it. She could talk in detail about Colombian emeralds, cornflower-blue Kashmir sapphires, Burmese rubies (O those Mogok mines, with stones the color of pigeon's blood).

"Well, it's special," said Tourneau. "And we're serving it specially for you. This ice is from the time of Shakespeare. Or should I say Chaucer?"

"Really!" said Markovsky, eyes wide.

"Thank you," said Barber politely.

"Explain, please," I said.

"It's centuries old. Got it from an ice core from a drill rig at the Pole. The ice showed annual layers, like a tree ring. You can study past weather and pollution in it. The layers of particulate matter show when the Industrial Revolution began."

"Ever heard of black ice?" Markovsky asked Tourneau. "Ben, tell about black. No, first about blue."

Paduani, who knew a lot about ice, was sitting on Barber's right and, as usual on the PENGUIN, was wearing Navy blues which contrasted with Tourneau's Coast Guard khakis. The ship was rolling heavily.

"Blue's very hard and brittle," said Paduani. "Flakes like shards. Takes a while for it to melt even in the sun. Mostly it ablates, changes directly into vapor. It's tasteless and centuries old. Last time I was at Palmer we'd get blue when we went out into the harbor in a Zodiac, and we'd bring it back and use it in cocktails. We'd board a large chunk with bare hands. It was glistening, pockmarked, and very heavy. And slippery, and very cold. Blue is freshwater ice formed under great pressure, so it depressurizes while melting, and pops and crackles loudly, like Chinese firecrackers. At Palmer it comes from the masses of ice that calve off the ice piedmont with a roar like thunder, causing high swells that are sometimes dangerous when you're in a Zodiac. We'd go into a brashfield for it, where the ice looked as if it had gone through a blender. Some of the pieces were large. Size of a pickup truck. Others were the size of a man or a dog. One growler lay very low in the water and looked like ordinary ice, except that at one end it was black and stippled, the kind I'd heard about but never seen. As we started to pass that end I expected the black to turn as gray as the water. But as we went still further toward the icecliffs and I glanced back at the ice, it looked even blacker than before. I was startled. The stipples were unchanged, though."

"Of course, you're excluding ice with black volcanic matter," said Markovsky.

"Correct."

Markovsky was wearing a Brooks Brothers blue plaid cotton Nehru shirt, which I hadn't seen before. Barber and I hadn't dressed specially for the occasion.

"Any blue-eyed shags at Palmer?" Tourneau asked Paduani.

"Lots. And giant petrels. The petrels bark, and spit a very acidy saliva at you if you come too close to their nests."

"Will you Observation guys be very busy when you hit the Peninsula?" asked Tourneau.

"Let's face it," I said, "we'll make only pro forma visits."

"To what stations?"

"British, Argentine, Chilean, Russian, Polish. We're not about to poke around, look for serious breaches of the Antarctic Treaty, such as ecological fuckups. Nobody really expects us to discover flagrant breaches of the Treaty. Our job is to keep alive, for geopolitical reasons, Article VII regarding open inspection of Antarctic stations. The U.S. wants the article to serve as an important precedent for other international treaties, and to lever Russia on mutual inspection. The article may fall into abeyance if it isn't used regularly."

The ship lurched heavily. Tourneau excused himself and went to his private head. When he rejoined the table, I noticed he had replaced the Cartier citrine ring with another pinky one, probably also by Cartier—a massive, barrel-shaped, yellow-gold mounting containing a large, bezel-set amethyst (10 carats?) of a remarkable color, known as Siberian. The stone had a buff top; that is, it was a cab or cabochon; only its bottom was faceted. Each side of the mounting held three small bezel-set diamonds which, though they sparkled energetically, were upstaged by the rich, dark-grapejuice flashes escaping from the killer amethyst.

"Tourneau, you're a bird," I thought. "George Barber here, looking shy or glum for some reason, relishes Antarctic rocks, whereas you treasure pinky rings more suitable for Leelee." I was reminded of a cartoon. Two peahens are observing a peacock strutting his magnificent plumage for them. One of the peahens says, "Okay, cut the crap and show us your willie."

Had Tourneau gone to the head because the icebreaker's sudden, violent motion had upset his delicate tummy? Did he hoard a supply of pinky rings in the head? Did wearing them help quiet his tummy? George was eyeing the amethyst.

Tourneau suddenly returned to his head and emerged wearing still another pinky ring, which he had substituted for the amethyst ring. It was constructed of two parallel bars of 14K yellow gold (not 18K; 14K for strength), with a one-and-a-half-carat diamond bezel-set in platinum. It was the largest single diamond I had ever seen a man wear. When I asked to examine it, Tourneau, handing it to me, said it was D flawless, the top of the line in diamond quality. But I suspected, from my experience with Leelee's diamonds, that he was in error or exaggerating, for I thought I could make out bear piss (a faint yellow) in the stone. However, it wasn't the greatest light for examining diamond color properly.

"I get severe headaches in a rolling ship," said Tourneau. "Last year, when we took fifty-degree rolls, I had a headache that lasted four days. But I've been lucky. No loss of life at sea during my watch, except for the crewman who got electrocuted last year."

"Did you bury him at sea?" asked Markovsky.

"Today, with freezer capability, you keep the body until you reach home port. The vessel won't change deployment for a dead man, only for a condition hazardous to life and limb. We have a physician's assistant, with two years of medical school, and a medical corpsman, on board. They can handle most medical problems that arise during a deployment. The most common problems are dental. But if you broke a tooth, or had some other accident that exposed you to thermal sensitivity, there'd be little that could be done for you before the ship reached port. The ship wouldn't change deployment for you."

"Other than the crewman being electrocuted, have you had any unusual experiences on this vessel?" asked Markovsky.

"Last year, in the Peninsula region, we were beset after we went to the aid of a beset Argentine vessel. Ice conditions were so bad it was decided we would winter-over with a reduced crew. Normally the CO makes important decisions in the field without consulting headquarters. But in this case I was overruled. I thought evacuation of personnel should be delayed, that ice conditions might improve. But headquarters ordered me to begin evacuation. So evacuation personnel were divided into teams of four each, with a team leader. That way it was easier to manage the operation. Evacuees went by helicopter to a nearby Argentine station, then by C130 to Rio Gallegos in Argentina. Some got as far as Buenos Aires. Ice conditions changed, so we were able to free ourselves. We went north to retrieve the evacuees."

"What'll happen to this vessel eventually?" asked Paduani.

"There's a project in which, after being extensively overhauled and to some extent redesigned, she'll be allowed to be frozen into the Arctic ice for two years to drift over the North Pole for scientific purposes. After that she'll be scrapped. Trouble is, the project is being designed without sufficient consultation with the people who know her best—those who run her."

It was the oddest shipboard dinner I ever attended. Tourneau on his best behavior, trying to patch up his PR. And George Barber reticent, distant, almost shy. A bunch of strutting cocks, and George almost wimpy.

* * *

Fog and sea mist. Endless heavy rolling. The weather decks eerily silent except for our engines. Standing in the bow, Barber and I can make out nothing except the water close to the ship. I see him remove something from his parka pocket and study it.

"What's that?" I ask.

He hands it to me. It's a card. I suppose you could have called it a miniature construction.

"It's exquisite," I say. "Who made it?"

"Alyssa. My wife. Glad you like it. I'll tell her. She'll be very pleased. She made eighty of them last December to send to friends. No two alike."

"Eighty! Wow! It's a work of art."

"I agree. I wanted a record of them, so I spread them on the floor and photographed them before she mailed them. As I was leaving the house to come here I pocketed this one."

I study it. A little, off-white, rectangular board, heavy with rag. A small, rectangular, sealed plastic envelope containing wrinkled strips of reddish paper intermeshed with odd-shaped bits of shiny metallic paper, and bits of golden net-like tissue, and other, tiny odds and ends. The envelope is attached to the board by a single white thread, handled with a needle. Pasted beneath it is a ruby, horizontal, ragged, ribbon-like paper on which has been typed in black ink: "splendiferous new year." His wife's handwriting is as fine as her craftsmanship, as I can see on the back of the board, where she has written a brief note to an Ellen. "Would you like to see a picture of Alyssa?" asks Barber and shows me one. She's tall, lean, blond, pretty, and looks to be loving and intelligent.

"What does she do?" I ask.

"Magazine editor."

The weather clears by mid-afternoon.

"Mr. Barber's presence is requested on the bridge!" sounds the PA.

Barber goes to the bridge, where Tourneau, using binoculars on the port bridge wing, informs him that an immense tabular berg has been sighted, containing huge grottoes.

"The berg is about a hundred and forty feet high," says Tourneau. "The largest cavern, the central one, is about ninety feet high. Here, have a look. I plan to get the prow into it. It's good for the crew's morale to experience spectacular stuff. When we're close, if you go to the bow you'll snap terrific shots."

The PA announces the presence of a huge berg, and soon many men crowd the bow, Barber among them. They're mostly young men wearing Coast Guard khakis. Two wear white trousers, half-sleeve white shirts and white chef's caps. Barber is conspicuous in his red parka.

The berg, looking mysterious, magnetic and immensely power-ful, has a flat top so large you could set up camp and hike on it. It has craggy sides and Roman arches, the latter showing intense cobalts, pale blues and electric greens. Eight large grottoes on the side visible to us are varied in size. Some are high, deep, with gloomy recesses. The grotto supports, suggesting flying buttresses, rest on ice pedestals reflected in the crisping, vivid green water. Lavender cavern walls. The sea in places blue, in others black. The berg makes you want to come closer, closer, as if you're drawn by great magic, or by something horrific, like the one-eyed Cyclops, gobbler of men, drooling blood, legs, arms, skulls.

A pure-white snow petrel, skimming the water, enters the main grotto, whose ceiling gives the impression of being formed of plaster of paris that, while still soft, was slashed by a palette knife. I'm standing on the fore part of the deck just below the bridge as the prow heads for this grotto. Waves are slamming thunderously into it, forming high spray. Brash in the entrance indicates recent ice falls. I think of running to the bridge to warn Tourneau but decide it would be foolish to do so. A Southern Ocean skipper would be aware of it. A cobalt fissure above the grotto zigzags toward the berg's top, indicating that an ice mass may be ready to calve. As the prow draws nearer I see there's more brash in the grotto than I at first noticed—white brash on a black sea, the brash restless because the water in the grotto is heaving.

Shooting, still in the bow, working swiftly, Barber seems transfixed, like the men surrounding him, all of whom are staring in the same direction. I have become so very fond of him. Our sharing the motel room in Christchurch. The talks we had at McMurdo, on helos in the McMurdo region, on the ship in all weather. The late-night poker games. The midrats forays. The trips to the phone shack and PX. The deep-night excursions onto the fantail deck. Our mutual distrust and dislike of Tourneau.

I spot Kenny Yost in the bow crowd. He's one of three or four guys wearing whites. Thin, skinny figure. Long, lever-like arms and legs. Does he have enough body heat to stay there long? Abe Lincoln flies into my head. Lincoln was from Illinois, Yost is from New Hampshire—"Live Free Or Die."

How paradoxical life can be. Here in the Antarctic it clings desperately to the world. You can find it in suspended bacterial animation in the bottom of Dry Valley bore holes a thousand feet deep, frozen, waiting—for what? Resurrection? Yet it can also be so fragile. Footsteps in the wrong place can badly damage or destroy an ecosystem created over millennia.

I want to cry out and warn Barber to come away from there. And Yost too. Yost is just a kid, he hasn't had a life yet. But, idiotically, I'm afraid of appearing foolish or, worse, of crying chicken.

I descend to the fo'c'sle and try to make my way to the bow, but the bow is so crowded I can't get through. I turn, glance up for some reason at the port bridge wing and catch Tourneau staring at me with a Mona Lisa smile.

Men, clustered in the bow, shout in unison in the hope of bringing ice down from the cave walls or ceiling. Thoughts of the horns of Jericho and of the Jericho walls crashing down. The chanting has no visible effect, so cries are heard asking the captain to sound the ship's horn.

"The following horn will *not* signify an emergency. Repeat: will *not* signify an emergency," announces the PA.

The ship's horn utters a long, loud, shuddering blast. Still no avalanche. Men whistling. Men shouting in unison.

The prow begins to slide into the central grotto. Is Tourneau risking lives to show off? Whom is he trying to impress? Barber? Himself? I remember the Russian ship slipping away into fog, my being spooked by it, my deciding not to share the feeling with Barber. "Yes!" I think, "I was right!" I recall that cats sense earthquakes long before humans and go nuts. "I'm like a cat!" I think. "Something horrible is about to happen! Save him!"

"Barber! George Barber!" I shout with all my might. "Come back! *Now!* Yost! Yost! Come back!"

I'm drowned out by the general uproar.

Again I glance at the port bridge wing, as if forced to do so. Tourneau again staring at me, now with a strange and what I take to be malevolent grin. I think I see something flash on one of his hands. Is it a pinky ring? I can't be sure.

A large chunk of the inmost grotto wall suddenly collapses, setting up a powerful swell. Other large chunks follow. Men in the bow racing headlong aftward as men on the upper decks, seeing the possibility of ice action on the bow men, call for *more, more* of the ship's horn. General laughter.

Shoved by terrified scampering men, Barber stumbles and falls. A man falls on top of him, scrambles up, keeps going. Barber lies still. The prow starts backing out of the grotto.

Men on the upper decks cry, "More horn!"

Suddenly a large chunk of ice drops from the grotto's ceiling onto the bow, killing Barber and a crewman instantly.

Shouts of horror mixed with screams. Men crawling. Blood visible among the ice. Tourneau looking ashen, sick, but shouting commands. The ship's horn announcing an emergency. The prow clearing the berg. Men rushing forward to help. More blue ice falling, now into the churning black sea.

Yost stumbles over Barber, realizes who it is, tries to help him up, sees the condition of his head and backs off in shock. Oblivious of his extreme danger, he stares transfixed at his now bloody hands.

"He has George Barber's blood on his hands," I think. "He's killed George Barber."

"Yost! Yost! Come back!" I shout.

He whips around and glares at the port bridge wing. He and Tourneau exchange a brief glance. I doubt, under the circumstances, that Tourneau recognizes him. Yost's young face shows almost cartoon hatred. An enlisted man grabs Yost's arm and yanks him into a run away from the bow, causing Yost to stumble again and this time almost to fall. Again Yost glances at the port bridge wing, but Tourneau has disappeared, leaving the wing empty.

My heart is pumping so fast and hard I'm afraid I'm going to have an attack or a stroke. Something seems to be pressing insistently against my left forehead. Reaching up, I find it's an engorged vein.

My mind wants me to rush out of there but my legs won't budge. When I finally reach my rack and briefly sit down I realize I'm sweating profusely. I go to the brilliantly lit head and walk up and down in that confined space, feeling the vein now and then. The ship's vibrations feel stronger than ever. My brain is a riot of hot disordered thoughts. My face in one of the mirrors scares me. For a moment I don't recognize it. Maybe my eyes, which have seen too much, are disinterested in seeing well for a while.

"It's not important to see too well," my eye doctor once remarked to me.

He had a back like Tourneau's stooge. Facial skin tight, tan onionskin over powerful jaws. Soft, gentle, distant manner, with an ethereal smile: a man from a better planet. We usually mentioned his teenage daughter, the prize-winning horsewoman, and her two mares. It seemed at the time like a nice philosophical observation, though not one that would appeal to astronomers or astrophysicists. I dropped him when he prescribed lenses that were so thick I couldn't see through them. Bottle glass. Thoughts of James Thurber, blind, thick lenses. James Joyce. The eye doc lost it, I *had* to give up on him. I had never given up on Leora, although she absolutely refused to say she loved me. Maybe it was enough she acted as if she did, now and then. One of the oddest things about our relationship is that she was most affectionate, and most pleased with me, when I was down with some bug, had half my usual energy. She said she could handle me then, that that was when I was the most fun.

I imagine the injured being carried on stretchers to sick bay. The dead being slipped into body bags for removal to a freezer. A detail, wearing latex gloves, swabbing the bloody deck.

I think of Phyllis and Linda, my daughters. As I said earlier, the Barbers had no kids. I don't know why. "At least there's no child left fatherless," I think. I imagine being with Barber in the bow, and myself being killed by the ice—a sudden tremendous blow to the skull, my brains scattered—and Linda and Phyllis getting the news from Leelee. My nostrils go funny, my eyes grow wet. "Hey, you're safe," I think. "It's okay. It happened to him, not you." I'm a survivor. Like Tourneau, the icebreaker captain with the pinky rings, one of which has a killer amethyst. Neither of us got close to the bow, to the grotto of the beautiful berg slowly drifting northward to die in warmer waters. The berg has been sculpted by westerlies, fierce storms, huge waves of very salty water. The Southern Ocean is the most saline of the planet's seas.

The light in the head is now too intense. I step outside, close the door behind me and stand for a long time in darkness except for the single red bulb. I've been spared, I didn't even think to go out onto that bow. I'm a coward. At any rate I'm no hero. George Barber, dedicated to his work, was the hero and look what happened. Where was God when the ice fell? Fooling around with black holes? "Should I warn Tourneau about Yost?" I wonder. I shrug. "Not my ship. Not my watch. Not my call." I don't know how long I stand there. Nobody comes to use the head.

I make my way to Barber's rack and stare at it as if I expect to see him lying on it, or as if I had a hand in his death. Maybe if I shouted more urgently—. I think, "I should have shared my hunch with him about something terrible about to happen. He might have taken me seriously. It might have spared him. Why was I so chicken?" His wife's exquisite card flies into my head. Her name is Alyssa. He told me she was a magazine editor. During a phone call to her he spoke briefly and almost drily, yet I imagine they were close, saw things eye to eye. I feel now I have an authentic impression of her—quiet, reserved, dependable, faithful, unlikely to do fifty thousand prostrations in a month. Yet like Leelee she can also be extreme—eighty handmade cards in December! Eighty! No two alike! Is the card still in George's parka pocket? Who will tell her George has been killed? I go to my rack and lie down, my heart still pounding.

Did Tourneau see Yost's look? Did it sink in? Will Tourneau punish him for it? The look, which has gotten mixed up in my head with Tourneau's weird smile, haunts me, makes me wonder why I'm incapable of an emotion so extreme. I hate nobody, at least not like that, and, I judge, nobody hates me. Nor do I have contempt for anybody. I suspect I may have been an object of contempt from time to time to Leora if nobody else. How much does her fat portfolio have to do with my staying in that marriage? If we break up, will I miss her? It's been an odd voyage from the start. I need to wash my hands of it. I feel as if I might start hallucinating.

"Did you see what happened?" asks Markovsky in the gloom.

"Yeh. You?

"I was on the starboard fo'c'sle. I'm going to lie down. I feel sick."

"Anything I can do?"

"No thanks."

I think I can hear his body relaxing on his rack. And then, over the ship's many noises, I think I can hear him crying. Crying? He of the State Department? The elegant London shoes? The gold lighter? It's impossible, I'm imagining it. Poor damn Barber. I'm angry with him, I feel let down, I had looked forward to a cool friendship. Was mine the last friendly voice in his life? Where did the Grotto Berg calve from? The ice was heavy, blue. Two points of destiny, colliding in the ocean vastness. The Grotto Berg was visible for miles, luring Tourneau to Barber's destruction. The hatred on Yost's face is frightening. Was that how it looks in a psychiatric ward? How will Tourneau explain sticking his prow into that cavern? The ship seems to vibrate more than ever. Dumb prow, it drew too close, the grotto bit it. I think of Leelee and our girls and that I'll probably make it back to them. I badly need to cry but can't.

* * *

We resume course for the Antarctic Peninsula. We still have the nightly movies but Tourneau is no longer present. There's a remarkable drop in the guffaw level. I hear a rumor he's seasick, which sounds odd since we're currently hugging the pack ice south of us. The wardroom drapes aren't very active as inclinometers. He may well be sick, but not for Southern Ocean reasons is my guess. What's he thinking? Is he looking for a cover-up? Will he hard-nose his way out of the very bad spot he's in? Many men cried for more horn. Will they share his guilt? Occasionally, to my surprise, I find myself feeling sorry for him. His stooge, big-ass Sonny Peterson, present at the movies, is noticeably subdued and, at times, seems apprehensive. Carpenter, the XO, joins my dinner sitting. I try reading his face but find nothing new except sidelong worried glances. There's much wardroom gossip about what happened, but not in Carpenter's presence. At my dinner sitting you might think nothing unusual recently occurred, but afterwards, with the XO gone, presumably back to his cabin, you hear lots of over-heated speculation mixed with dogmatic opinions.

Yost is nowhere to be seen in the wardroom or in the wardroom area. Going to the wardroom galley for a cup of coffee, I'm waited on by the young enlisted man who told Barber that Yost was in sick bay.

"Where's Yost?" I ask.

"Sick bay, sir."

"A second time?"

"Yes sir."

"Why?"

He lowers his voice. "CO says he's a whistleblower and disobedient. I don't know what the CO's problem is. Kenny gets along with everybody. He's a neat guy. The CO's got a hair up his ass about Kenny."

Remembering vividly how Barber's conversation with Yost had been overheard, or recorded, or whatever, I glance around the crowded room and find no clear reason to be worried about my privacy. I try to spot any bugging device in the galley and to check the young man's white clothes for a visible device.

"Can you give Yost a message for me?"

"No problem."

"Say I wish him well."

"Yes sir."

"How's he taking being in sick bay?"

"He don't say much."

"What happens if he leaves?"

"Without permission? They'd put him in irons, I guess."

"He's just a kid. Things are stacked against him. Tell him to stay out of trouble."

"Heard of stigmata, sir?"

"Of course."

"You believe in stigmata?"

"Certainly."

"So do I. Some of the guys say Kenny has performed a miracle."

"How?"

"In his hands, where the nails went through."

"Where's sick bay?"

"Near the ham shack."

"I'm on my way."

Sick bay is a lot smaller than I expected, and it smells of midrats. Yost is sitting on a rack. Looking very surprised to see me, he stands up.

"I came to see your famous hands," I say.

He smiles. "I guess I'm famous now, at least on this ship," he says, "at least among my buddies."

He holds them up for me, palms first, then turns them over. The dark areas on both sides don't take much imagination to believe they're the leftovers of severe wounds. Close examination shows no obvious signs of fakery. However, the light isn't great.

"When did it happen?"

"Last night, in my sleep. I was scared when I first saw them this morning."

"Thanks," I say. "I believe them. And I believe in you. I wish you well. Try to stay out of trouble."

"Yes sir," he says.

We shake hands and I return to the wardroom and my coffee.

Gone is Tourneau's nightly poker game. Which leaves Paduani socially afloat, as if he's been abandoned in a kind of no-man's-land. He withdraws from chitchat with Markovsky and me. I no longer feel part of a team. The wardroom goings-on seem remote to me, as though I'm a visitor from another planet. I'm struck by the fact that all these guys are behaving as if their lives are substantial, as solid as granite, whereas in truth, as it seems to me now, we're all like the Grotto Berg, relentlessly heading toward the waters waiting to melt us.

* * *

Weird, foggy weather, almost like a whiteout. I'm on the helo deck because it's painful for me to be inside, in the wardroom, in TOQ, in the head, where I still hear George Barber's voice and still see his prominent Adam's apple and his brown, unrelentingly piercing eyes and still, for some reason, remember his near-scalding in Christchurch. I spot two figures silently wrestling close to the very low gunnel. Should I try to intervene? Should I shout something? A warning? A cry for help? A primeval, guttural rush of air out of my lungs and throat? If I intervene bodily in that primitive wrestling I may myself fly over the gunnel, and that will be the end of me too, as it was of George Barber.

One figure suddenly knees the other's groin. The latter hunches over in pain. The first figure heaves him overboard, then scuttles out of sight. Has he seen me? Am in danger? Only then do I have a hunch the man overboard is Jack Tourneau and that the fleeing figure is young Kenny Yost from New Hampshire with the thin, vulnerable neck and lever-like legs. *Live Free Or Die*, his state license plate said.

Heart pounding, mind still preoccupied with George Barber alive and George Barber dead, I return to the wardroom, where I keep my suspicions to myself.

Who am I to sit in judgment on Kenny Yost?

THE LEFT EYE
CRIES FIRST

ONE

The following events occurred shortly before the Soviet Union self-destructed. Mikhail Gorbachev was still in power at the time.

It was near dawn early in April, and dapper Sid Little, sixty-three, of Roslyn, Long Island, an early-retired attorney who had very recently had a second and glorious bar mitzvah, was dreaming: he was walking in the Village, when he learned that Dick Gallagher, a retired AT&T minor executive who had Parkinson's and whom he hadn't seen in years, had died. And then he was in Dick Gallagher's spacious Village apartment on Confederate Street, and a stout, middle-aged, Slavic-looking woman he didn't know was rummaging here and there.

"Dick has such a large statuary," she remarked to Sid Little.

Sid Little woke up perturbed. He felt guilty toward Dick because of Dick's disease, because of Dick's death (in the dream), because he hadn't seen him in a long time, and because he himself was still remarkably healthy for his age. (Genes and luck. And a little treadmill now and then. And a little spaziergang, a little stroll.) Had Dick really died?

"Give him a call, check it out," thought Sid Little.

But probably Nora Gallagher, Dick's second wife, would answer the phone, and Sid had a problem with that. He had met Nora only once, but in a way that was unforgettable. He was dining in their duplex apartment, when she suddenly reached out with long fingers and put some wet food into his mouth. She did that to him, to meticulous Sid. And then she did it a second time. And a third. That was chutzpa. That was heavy trading on his long friendship with Dick. In his whole sixty-three years no woman except his mom, not even Doris, his half-Jewish wife, let alone a full shiksa, had taken that liberty with him. Doris, who hadn't been present at the incident, which had become famous in Sid's close circle, had always been skeptical that it had actually occurred. The half-shiksa in her had possibly been prejudiced in favor of the full shiksa's good manners.

Dick was Irish Catholic. Nora was Swedish Protestant. Blond, cool, speaking with an accent, where'd she pick up a habit like that, forcing a virtual stranger to taste her long, wet fingers? And tall, lanky Dick, with his close-cropped, thick Lincoln beard, with touches of gray, had eyed the scene with an ironic smile. Disparity everywhere. Dick's Catholicism. Nora's Protestantism. Doris's half-breed beginnings. (But she had adopted the Jewish faith.) And Sid Little's uneasy Jewishness.

Nevertheless, Sid phoned Dick Gallagher's number, and, sure enough, Nora answered. Recalling her height, her blondness and her bold smiles with their brilliant uneven teeth, Sid identified himself.

"How'd you come to call me?" Nora whispered in an intimate tone.

As if he'd call *her*.

"I called to see how you two are doing," he lied.

"It's ESP," whispered Nora. "I've been meaning to write to you."

And then she related a tale of horror, punctuated by spells of weeping, and it unnerved Sid Little to hear such a cool, tall, Stockholm blond cry like that. One evening a couple of months ago, when she came home from work at the literary agency on Madison Avenue, Dick complained of pains in his chest and suggested they check them out at nearby St. Vincent's Hospital, where, Nora said, Dylan Thomas, the great Welsh poet, had died one dark night, finally done in by alcohol. She asked Dick if she should call a cab. "Why don't we walk," said Dick, known for his macho. But on the way he started to buckle, and they made it only with a male pedestrian's help. And Dick had a heart attack in the ER. And afterwards the doctor told Nora privately that Dick had probably had other attacks but hadn't noticed them because of the pain of his Parkinson's. And so Dick had been hospitalized ever since, first at St. Vincent's and now at Union Hospital in Chelsea, where he alternated between bed and a wheelchair.

Listening intently to the story, Sid Little, feeling panicky, sensed it was also about himself, that it was telling him his own time was almost up, and he recalled something Mark Twain had once said. "Chaucer is dead. Shakespeare is dead. And I'm not feeling too good myself."

"Sid, the Richard we knew and loved is no longer here," said Nora. "Richard died in the ER. It would have been merciful if he had been allowed to stay dead. But the ER doctor, the idiot, said, 'His vital signs are all good.' And so, using high tech, they brought him around. So Richard now often hunches in a wheelchair, his eyes tightly shut. And sometimes he asks me, 'Why is it so hard to die? Can't you get me a cyanide pill?' The doctor gives him a drug to keep him from becoming too rigid, because if he becomes very rigid the nurses will refuse to help him. He's heavy. They have their backs to consider. Also, if his mouth becomes rigid he won't be able to swallow. A couple of weeks ago, planning to kill himself, he stopped eating and drinking. At first the staff threatened to force-feed him. Then, worrying about a lawsuit for assault and battery, they drugged him and fed him intravenously. Before this trouble started he refused to sign a Living Will. And now he refuses to sign anything, and refuses to be cremated. *My* ashes will be scattered over my beloved Manhattan. Kevin, Richard's younger brother, a handsome, charming, Irish ladies' man, visited him last week, and Richard was horribly abusive. He shouted, 'Get the fuck out of here!' But you he loves, Sid. He saved all your Israel postcards. And he tried never to miss a program dealing with the Holocaust. He used to say there's great rapport between Jews and the Irish."

"So what's the prognosis?" asked Sid.

"Terrible. Terrible. Sid, please write an obit and send it to me. I'll send it on to the *Times*."

"An obit?"

"Yes."

"Nora."

"What?"

"I can't do that."

"Why not?"

"He's still alive, for God's sake."

"You owe him one."

"Why me? I'll visit him."

"Because you're very articulate. And you loved him. And he loved you."

"You talk as if he's dead."

"See for yourself. Third floor. Union Hospital. But write the obit for the *Times*."

"I'll think about it."

"What's bugging her?" wondered Sid as he hung up. "What makes her think he's worth one?"

The thought of scratching together some materials about Dick's life irritated him. Though he liked and admired Dick, Dick's life didn't seem worth a *Times* obit. Sid's own life seemed a more likely candidate.

Anyway, the next day he drove his new, shiny white Lexus from the Island to Manhattan, parked the car in a Chelsea garage and headed for Union Hospital. He had bought the Japanese car as a matter of course, replacing a six-year-old Camry. On the other hand, given the Holocaust, under no condition would he have purchased a German car, though he admired the BMW, not to mention the Mercedes.

Would Dick be abusive to him, as he had been to his own younger brother? If he was, how should he, Sid, handle it? Philosophically? But what if Dick told *him* to get the fuck out of there? How had the brother handled it? Nora had forgotten to say. Sid expected to visit the old Dick Gallagher, lanky, Lincoln-bearded, and so Dick's sea change frightened him. On spotting the gaunt, haggard, un-Irish-looking stranger propped up in bed, hair wildly uncombed, eyes looking nowhere, Sid, convinced he had entered the wrong room, retreated to the corridor, heart pounding. But a strong inner voice said, "Remember who you are. You're Sid Little. And it's not Sid Little's habit to confuse hospital room numbers."

Which was true enough, for he was a man upon whom facts could depend. He had worked in negligence law for a law firm and, later, in compensation cases for the State of New York. And he had attained a high degree of authority, becoming a compensation-case judge (a compensation-case referee, actually). Of middle height, with a dignified, affluent, quietly authoritative air, and with an aquiline, jolly look, he appeared to be well preserved, as if he had taken good care of himself. His mouth usually gave the impression he smiled often in an empathetic way, suggesting he was on pleasant terms both with his body and his God. But now it looked frightened, and out of character for a senior citizen dressed in a charcoal gray suit with vest, with clocked silk hose to match, and with new black shoes.

"That really is Dick Gallagher in there," he thought, and forced himself to enter the room again. And the voice said, "Thank God this isn't happening to me, to Little Sid Little," a reference to his having been called, by certain friends long, long ago, some of whom were already dead, Little Sid Little after Little Jack Little, a minor Thirties vaudevillian: joker, pianist, baritone: in that order.

Dick Gallagher was now hawk-nosed, ashen, and his hospital gown, tied loosely around him, revealed emaciated hairy shoulders, and a hairy chest with sagging pectoral muscles whitened by talcum. And here were his arms, as gorilla-hairy as ever, but now with hanging skin and flesh. He had apparently been eating at the stainless steel tray in front of him, for glistening food bits clung to his mouth and chin. The calves of Sid's short legs twitched in their desire to run.

"Dick! Sid Little! Hiya doin'?" he said, feeling that something awful was going to happen to himself.

Dick's face showed no surprise at this unexpected visit. "Fighting hard," he replied, then added something lengthy.

But Sid couldn't make it out, because Dick had barely opened his mouth. And he had spoken in a guttural tone, and with odd pauses, and with a tremor, yet his voice was deep, almost resonant. His eyes, not much larger than slits, were fixed on Sid's. The heavy, yellowish, owl-like lids were barely open. At times the left eye shut tightly while the right one kept a close vigil. His mouth too was a slit. All in all, Dick Gallagher seemed to be wearing a mask suggesting he was a native of Outer Mongolia.

Sid moved from Dick's left, the window side, to Dick's right, adjacent to his roommate. The roommate's condition caused a further churning in Sid's stomach. The middle-aged, gray-haired man, lying on his side, was apparently in a coma. His forehead was frightfully bruised, and his mouth was toothless, and one hand and arm were heavily bandaged. A pretty, brown-haired, middle-aged woman sat near the foot of the bed, reading a hardcover book.

"What horrible things happen to us humans!" thought Sid.

Dick, staring at him, said something softly and without any apparent motion of his lips.

"Hit me again?" said Sid.

Dick again murmured something.

"They're drugging you?" Sid asked, leaning forward and staring at Dick's bluish lips.

Was he reading the imminence of death in them? He should have felt very close to his old friend in the latter's time of need. Instead, though his intentions were good, he felt himself distancing, as if Dick had a dread and catching disease: bubonic plague, which had wiped out a third of Europe in the Middle Ages; the latest TB mutant, resistant to antibiotics; or a variant of streptococcus, the so-called flesh-eating bug, whose enzymes digested human muscle and fat.

"The leader of the clinic," said Dick Gallagher. "He's a Parkinson's patient. Indicted for murder. He wanted to buy a trinket for a couple of million bucks for his girl friend. [Unintelligible]"

"Murder?" asked Sid.

"If you can't hear *me*, and I can't hear *you*, there's no point in continuing the conversation," said Dick abruptly, staring icily at Sid.

Sid Little was startled. Was the visit going to be aborted so soon? He thought of Dick's younger brother and half expected to be ordered to get the fuck out of there. Had he, Sid, a retired New York State compensation-case judge, driven all the way from Roslyn, on the Island, for nothing?

"Old pal," Dick Gallagher murmured suddenly, affectionately, and warmly shook Sid's hand.

Dick's fingers, wet and sticky from the food he had been handling, reminded Sid of Nora Gallagher's fingers in his mouth.

"What would he think if I told him Nora asked me to write his obit? And for the *Times*, no less?" Sid wondered as he reached into a pocket for a tissue.

"Are you in much pain?" he asked.

"Tremendous. It's exacerbated by the conditions in this hospital. The hospital doesn't want to reduce the pain. They claim that with pain you live a little longer. But life isn't worth living this way. And the longer is very little."

"Cogently put," thought Sid. "When do you think you'll be leaving?" he asked.

"Tonight. I'm going to be in court for a week. I'm going to press the case for murder against this son of a bitch. He killed two people for two million bucks. Nora doesn't know whose side she's on. I'm on her side. [Unintelligible] The fact that she became a porno queen is not something I hold against her. Except [unintelligible] she can pass on AIDS to me. If she *has* AIDS. So basically I'm on her side. And basically I think she's on my side. How old are you? You used to be a lot younger."

"I'm a very old party," said Sid. "That's what Somerset Maugham said about himself in *The New Yorker* a long time ago."

"I want to get dressed," said Dick. "I need to be taken to my hotel. Get the head nurse. They say they'll come in a little bit, and an hour goes by. Phone the hotel. The Plaza Hotel. [Unintelligible] Tell them you have the right, under the law, to call your clinic and this number. Insist on being heard. If it takes you more than five minutes, come back. No more than five minutes. Go right now!"

Feeling Dick's hostility, and feeling his own rising to the surface, and not wanting to deal with either right now, Sid went to the men's room, where he took a leak, then strolled up and down the corridor.

"Bad news," said a heavyset nurse to him, who had seen him emerge from Dick's room. "He wants to mobilize the world. One day he tells me, 'You know, the doctor, he murdered ten patients.' I said, 'Where'd you get this idea?' 'In the *Times*.' Go ahead, argue. But today he's talking, and that's important."

Sid rejoined Dick Gallagher.

"You know, I was attached homosexually," Dick said. "To this patient next to me. He has AIDS. So now I'm infected. Call the Plaza. Say you're calling for me. Say you're calling for Dick Gallagher and [unintelligible]."

A nurse entered.

"Have you finished eating, Mr. Gallagher?" she asked.

"I want a telephone number that works," said Dick.

"I'll have to call upstairs," she said.

When she raised Dick's gown from his feet up to his waist to change the penis dressing (Dick's penis had a flesh-colored tape around it), Sid was shocked to see how wasted Dick's legs were. Dick's testicles were loose, large, purplish.

"That's heez seekness, you know?" the nurse whispered to Sid as she was leaving the room. "Sometimes heez here, sometimes no."

"It'll take at least an hour and a half," said Dick. "[Unintelligible]"

"Dick, where is it most painful?"

"Everywhere. Take this off me."

"What?" asked Sid.

"Everything. [Unintelligible] I'm never off. Give me the phone." There was no phone visible. "[Unintelligible] I want you to go right now. It'll take you only two minutes. If it takes more than two minutes, come back. Right now. Get going. Go and do it right now. Go and do it right this minute. The phones are not working, right? So go down to the lobby and say you're entitled to make a call. They never take care of anything. They never do. That's why I want you to call the Plaza. [Unintelligible] Tell them about the porno queen. Go! Right now! [Unintelligible] Use a phone booth. Nora's not crazy. It's her right. It bothers me that she's a porno queen, but that's beside the point. It bothers me personally, but legally she has a right to [unintelligible]. Her life style is different from mine. If she wants to sleep with fifty men in one night, that's *her* business. [Unintelligible] It won't take you more than fifty seconds. Otherwise you'll never get there. Will you make the call right now? But immediately. [Unintelligible] Follow me? Do it fast. [Unintelligible] Plaza Hotel. Room Two O Three. [Unintelligible] To tell the porno queen story. That's all you need. The operator will then know [unintelligible]. Room Six O Three. [Unintelligible] And it's your right. And if they don't do it, you give it just for the record. You'll be back in two minutes."

Dick studied Sid Little penetratingly. Sid felt a desire to say something sharp.

"Hello, Sid."

Nora Gallagher, blond, and wearing white clothes, had entered the room.

"Hello, Nora."

"How good of you to come. Darling, why haven't they combed your hair?"

She went to Dick's side, got a comb out of her black leather handbag and worked at civilizing his clumps and strands.

"Has he been telling you I'm a porno queen?" she asked Sid. "Darling," she said to Dick, "I wasn't lucky enough to have fifty. The most I ever had in one night was thirty-five."

"Thirty-five, fifty, what does it matter?" said Dick. "It's your life style, and I respect it."

"Darling, they didn't wipe your mouth, and they know you have a visitor." She wiped away Dick's food bits with a cloth napkin. "Darling, Sid and I are going into the corridor for a little chat. We'll be right back."

In the corridor she asked Sid, "Have you given more thought to the obit?"

"It won't work for me, Nora."

"Why not?"

"I don't write obits. I'm not a newspaper man."

"Do it. Do it, Sid."

"For God's sake, Nora. Dick's in that room, still alive."

"You're stubborn, Sid. I didn't understand that about you before."

Sid Little let the matter drop. Saying good-bye soon afterwards, he took another leak and headed for the garage, his buzzing head seeming to swell. However, the thought of imminently driving his new, white Lexus, which ran so smoothly, almost so sweetly, calmed him a little.

About a month later, at the beginning of May, he received a call from Nora, who said, "Sid, I have good news and bad. Which do you want first?"

"Good," he replied, recalling the taste of her long, manicured fingers.

"Richard's been home almost a week. Thank God, he's lucid again."

"That's great! And the bad?"

"In addition to Parkinson's, he now has stomach cancer."

"Good God!"

"*Now* will you write the *Times* obit?"

"Nora. Take it easy. I've already explained why I can't."

"I don't understand why not. All I'm asking for is a small *Times* obit. Which makes even more sense now that he has cancer."

"I'm sorry."

"Where's your humanity? Sid, you disappoint me. I'm starting to wonder if you're the broad, generous, humane person everybody says you are."

"I'm just me. Little Sid Little," Sid said.

The call soon ended.

"Obit, obit. She's going to drive me crazy with her *Times* obit," he thought, recalling the wet food between his shocked lips.

As if her call wasn't enough, the very same afternoon he received one from Dick himself, who said, "Nora told you I hit the jackpot? Parkinson's. A heart attack. And now stomach cancer."

It took a moment for the meaning of the words to get a hold of Sid, because Dick was speaking through clenched jaws.

"Dick, I can't tell you how sorry I am," said Sid, feeling guilty about his own excellent health, health that had begun to feel strange to him, as though it was somebody else's.

"I keep asking Nora to get me something that will finish me off," said Dick. "But she's a tough fighter. She refuses to accept my reality. She believes I'm going to recover, and that we'll travel to exotic places, even Siberia. Old buddy, can you get me something, at least a handful of sleeping pills?"

"I'm afraid not, old buddy."

"Old buddy, there's no point in my continuing like this. The quality of my life is unbelievable. I want to die. But I don't know how to accomplish it. I spend most of my days in a wheelchair now."

"Do you get outdoors?"

"Only when Nora or a nurse pushes me around the block. Still, I'm lucky, because we have our little garden, which she keeps up faithfully. Despite the Village air, the white roses are fragrant. And I'm lucid. At least I have that. But I'm such a terrible burden. Nora should have a life of her own. The only solution for me is dying. Will you visit me, old buddy?"

"You better believe it."

"Soon?"

"You bet."

"Bring Doris this time. I miss her. She's a fun lady. And so easy to look at."

"Of course."

"Good. Good."

And so, the following week, the Sid Littles visited the Dick Gallaghers in their expensive, duplex Village apartment. And Sid, happening to glance at Doris during the first few moments of the visit, noticed how pale she was, and frightened-looking, and assumed she was stunned by the changes in Dick Gallagher, whom she hadn't seen in two or three years. And it was almost as if Nora, sensing Doris's reaction, wished to spare her, for she quickly led her into the garden, which was a flight below, leaving Sid and Dick to chat in the spacious living room with its large fireplace, where Dick sat on an oak chair.

Dick was wearing a purple dressing gown with gold threads, and blue pajamas. A thin gray blanket, which he adjusted occasionally to protect his once powerful but now meager shoulders, covered his body like a tent. His mouth was screwed up, as if he was tasting a lemon.

"How horrifically and rapidly he's changed," thought Sid. "He used to be attractive-looking. Now he's gaunt and bloodless. But his beard looks as healthy as ever."

"Are you cold, Dick?" he asked.

"I'm warm enough. But my temperature is 96.5."

"Is that good?"

"Nothing's good for me any more, Sid."

"I'm sorry to hear you say that."

"I don't like to hear it myself, old buddy. But it's true. Still, there's *some* progress. At least I don't have to use the bile bag any more."

Although he knew nothing about bile bags, Sid had a frightening vision of Dick using one.

"I feel so sorry for poor Nora. I'm such a burden," Dick said slowly, haggard eyes downcast.

Nora and Doris entered the room and sat down.

"Doris, you have such a lovely figure. How do you stay so slim?" Nora asked.

Doris Little, avoiding glancing at Dick Gallagher, laughed loudly, blushing.

"I know how to hide the bad places," she said shyly.

"What bad places?"

"Oh, they're there, believe me," said Doris softly.

She seemed vulnerable, almost pathetic, though her brass-golden hair was cut short and looked mannish, and though she had a youthful, athletic figure. Her lavender blouse had a subtle, pleasing pattern. Her cuffless trousers were a deep, rich brown. Her brown shoes were of alligator skin.

"I love your leather pants," said Nora. "They're so soft. And they fit you beautifully."

"I got them off the rack," Doris whispered.

"Did you have them altered?"

"No. I was lucky." Doris laughed loudly again.

"And I love your sapphire ring. It's stunning. Where did you get it?"

"At a flea market," Doris whispered again. "South of Lambertville. In New Jersey."

"Flea market? Is it genuine?"

"It's a Burmese sapphire. 2.4 carats. With two thirty-point diamonds. All set in platinum. We have the appraisal papers that came with it. An expert in Philadelphia."

"And where did you find the onyx and silver one? Also at a flea market? I like the onyx triangle. And the gold bars on each side of the onyx soften the effect."

"Sid had it made for me by a jeweler he knows in Scarsdale. The man told Sid the triangle is a feminine motif and that dikes use it as a symbol for themselves." Once again Doris laughed loudly. "The upper part of the inside is scalloped out. Raw silver, nice to look at."

"And what's that ring you're wearing?" Nora asked Sid.

"He bought it to celebrate his second bar mitzvah," said Doris. "It's rose gold. The stone is fool's gold. I said, 'Sid, how can you, a faithful Jew, buy fool's gold to celebrate your second bar mitzvah?' He said, 'Because it reminds me of the great open spaces of the raw American West, and the gold rush, and mining.' I said, 'Really?' He only smiled."

"So why *did* you choose fool's gold?" Nora asked Sid.

"To be honest with you, I'm no longer sure," said Sid seriously.

"You haven't explained why you recently had the second bar mitzvah," said Nora. "I'm so sorry we couldn't make it. But Richard—"

"So are we!" cried Doris.

"Well," said Sid after a pause, glancing at Dick, whose eyes were closed, "about a year ago I asked myself, 'What's the meaning of my life? And where has it gone? And where is it going?' And I started to realize that life is nothing without renewal. And that renewal requires repetition, but with a variation. I had married Doris twice. So I decided to have a bar mitzvah twice. I had been attending services regularly. And kids had come up and been bar mitzvahed. And it sort of struck me. Also, you had some of the congregation, the older men, reciting the haftorah, which is the gravamen of the bar mitzvah ceremony. And I got to thinking . . . well . . . maybe I should do it. It's part of my recent questing, if you will. As my time grows shorter, I look back more and more, obviously because there's not as much time to look forward to.

"Anyhow, while debating with myself, I ended up with a couple of operations—gallbladder, prostate—which were a sort of block, if you will, to this thing. And I guess as time went on, I was looking forward to my sixty-third birthday—fifty years after my first bar mitzvah. What should I *do* on my sixty-third birthday? Run a party? That was nice, but a little bit self-congratulating. Now, Doris had a *bas* mitzvah when she was fifty-four, and this may have inspired me to have a *bar* mitzvah. There were thirteen ladies who took a course for two years, and their class met once a week, and they were taught the haftorah there. It's a part of the Torah which is recited each Sabbath, the thing that's recited in trope—chanting. Doris's mother is Gentile, and at one point in her life Doris converted to Judaism. Of the thirteen women in her bas mitzvah class, she was the only one who had converted. Our daughter, Harriet, went to an orthodox camp for years, and she too had a bas mitzvah—'to reaffirm my faith,' as she said."

"My mom was thrilled when I was doing my bas mitzvah," said Doris loudly, "because, as she said, 'This is something that *you* want to do. And it's a growth experience for you.' *Her* mom was brought up in a convent, and she had so strict a background that she didn't bring it forth to her children. Actually, the way I found out I was Jewish was interesting. We were never aware of religion, one way or the other. But we did have a woman taking care of us. My mom thought she'd like to go to work at one time. And this woman would go to church. So, coming home from school one day, I had nothing to do. And I went to church with this woman. And when I came home, my dad said, 'Go wash your face. You've got dirt on your forehead.' I said, 'That's not dirt. That's Ash Wednesday.' So he turns to my mom and he says, 'That's *your* doing.' She says, '*My* doing? First I hear about it!' And so that day I knew I was Jewish. And then, the other time, in school, the teacher was taking count. And in those days they said, 'How many Christians? How many Jews?' And she had counted wrong. And finally it dawned on her. 'Is there anyone standing twice?' And of course *I* stood twice. I was half-Jewish and half-Christian."

"Doris's was a mass affair," explained Sid. "A mass bas mitzvah. Thirteen women in Port Washington. Which reminds me. We were on a cruise, Doris and I, ten years ago, whatever. And we were in Canada. And there was this gentleman on the cruise who was a priest. As a matter of fact, he's now a monsignor, a fellow named Tom Finn. A lovely Irishman. I think some of these Irishmen are the loveliest guys in the world. The right Irishman—and that goes especially for you, Dick—you can't beat, as far as I'm concerned."

Dick opened his eyes, smiled wanly, and shut them again.

"And I thought," Sid continued, "'What's a priest doing on this trip? Is he taking care of Catholics? Or what? There's more than Catholics on this trip.' So I asked him. And the priest said, 'Oh, I'm like a chaplain. If I go and act as chaplain, I get to be a freebie.' So one day we get a bulletin of the day's activities, and it says, 'This afternoon Reverend Thomas Finn is running an ecumenical renewal of marriage vows for anybody who's interested.' So we went and got remarried. It was a nice ceremony, with champagne. We have pictures of it. The priest handled it beautifully. There were all kinds of people—Protestants, Jews, Catholics. Nothing in there that could be objectionable to *any*body.

"Another thing that may have influenced me to have a second bar mitzvah was this. Our daughter was working in Canada and living in a town there, and she invited us to come up for a weekend. This town had some Jewish people. She said, 'Do you want to go to services Saturday morning?' I said, 'By all means.' So we went there, and they had a mass both *bar* mitzvah and *bas* mitzvah, because up in Canada the Jewish people often lived in communities in which there weren't enough men to form a quorum, a minion, to conduct the service. Ten men. And so many of the men were *not* bar mitzvahed even though they may have come out of an orthodox family. It was a beautiful service."

Sid spoke quickly, in staccato, and his voice was deep and resonant. He was clearly used to being flooded by words, and enjoyed unburdening himself while basking in articulateness.

"You know," said Doris Little, "I had it in the back of my mind that I didn't want somebody some day telling me I can't be buried in a Jewish cemetery. So I converted. There were two reasons why I converted. The other was, my daughter was going with a Jewish young fellow. And the young man's mother felt. . . . Well, you know. She questioned if I was Jewish. So because of that I thought, 'Listen. I don't want to take any chances.' So one day I went to the rabbi, and I said, 'Rabbi, —'"

"You've got to remember, we lived there many years," Sid interrupted. "The rabbi had no thought that there was anything but a hundred percent Jewish blood on both sides. One day, for whatever reason, Doris decides she wants to make it all kosher. So she goes in to see the rabbi. And she says, 'I have something serious to talk with you about.' And he says, 'What is it?' And she says, 'I want to change my religion.' He's stunned. He doesn't know what she's talking about."

"The rabbi says, 'Why would anyone want to give up Judaism?'" said Doris. "I was just thinking. When Harriet went to this orthodox camp, she went there because I was hospitalized for a nervous breakdown. For two years, I was hospitalized. And Sid was such a good boy. He never looked at another woman. At least I don't think he did. He visited me regularly once a week, and brought me miniature carnations because he knows I like them. With great green sprays of stuff, and tiny buds. And when I came out I said, 'This child is spouting Hebrew. They're taking my child away from me. I'm not part of this.' It was like somebody kidnapped my daughter. And it wasn't until after I studied that I felt, 'Well, nobody can tell *me* I'm not Jewish, because I know the rules, I know more now.' Now I go to the temple. I sing the songs. I attend the rabbi's class. And I find it very very stimulating. I converted because I wanted to be buried in the cemetery next to Sid. And I didn't want anybody telling me what I felt. And what I didn't feel. I thought I might as well get this over and done with. So I go to the mikvah. It's an awful large bathtub. With a lot of buoyancy. It has louver doors. And the rabbi is on the other side of the doors. I take all my clothes off. You can't have any nail polish on. Any makeup of any kind. Not only that. This matron is there. And she. . . . It's a funny thing. I never did this before. The buoyancy lifts you up. And my tush touches the side wall of the tub. And she says, 'That's no good. You have to do it over. You have to completely submerge and touch nothing.' So then, when I come out of this tub, she says, 'Do you have any hair on you?' I said, 'Only in the normal places.' She meant that I had stepped out of the pool, and if I had a hair on my foot, I'd have to go and do it over again."

"She had three rabbis there," explained Sid. "All checking her out. And did the matron examine your hands to see if you had nail polish?"

"You bet," said Doris. "And she has you lift your feet. She looks at the soles. One rabbi is saying some prayers. And I have to answer while this is going on. The other two are in a room, where afterwards they give you wine. And have you sign a certificate reaffirming your faith. Very orthodox women have to go every month to purify themselves. Before you have sex with anybody, you have to have this ritual. My dad came to visit one day. And we were going to temple. He says, 'That's okay. I'll go with you.' So we're having a Jewish study class. And my dad gets up to go to the men's room. I said to Sid, 'Quick! Go after him!' Sid said, 'He's going to take a leak. Why do I have to go after him?' I said, 'Just do it!' And sure enough, my dad, he's in the temple, and he's talking to somebody in the men's room. And while peeing, he's saying, 'I don't go for all this stuff.'"

"Her dad had this talent," explained Sid. "No matter where you went, he managed to say the wrong thing."

"So I had *this* to contend with too," Doris said. "Not only were my mom and sister beautiful. And I wasn't. But they said I was just like my dad, I was sure to say the wrong thing at the right time."

"Two other events may have influenced me," said Sid. "One night I dreamed I was praying with my bar mitzvah classmates. And we were all kneeling. And each of us had his face in his hands. But I peeked. And I saw a large, sparsely furnished room. And God was sitting alone at a table. He looked so simple. So simple. But his beautiful hands, clasped on the old, uncovered table, radiated a shimmering blue haze. The man guarding the door invited me in. He was Moses. But instead of looking powerful, like in Michelangelo's statue, he looked pale, shaky. And he said to God, 'At last somebody understands my message.' And then I saw that he had been irradiated. And I understood that his message was, that he was denying his divinity. And the divinity of Jesus, another important Jew. And then one day I was watching a documentary about Kristallnacht. And I saw these SS guys beating up Jews. And it wasn't wartime. And it wasn't some forgotten little Polish village. It was right there in German cities. Germany: height of culture, civilization. And I suddenly felt very close to the Holocaust. I began to read. And I followed a gunpowder trail of anti-Semitism right up to, and past, Martin Luther's call to burn down synagogues."

There was a long silence.

"And so what's the spiritual meaning of your second bar mitzvah?" asked Dick, opening his eyes and studying Sid intently.

"Dick, you have to go into my approach to religion. I'm not a believer in the mysticism of it. I'm more attached to Judaism as a cultural, historical thing. I don't put people down who *have* that kind of feeling. But I don't get involved with the supernatural in this business. Second bas and bar mitzvahs are becoming fashionable. Many men and women repeat the ceremony because they believe they went through it by rote as adolescents, without understanding what they were doing. They need more than rote and ritual for their emotional and spiritual life. Dick, I'm not unaware of the slick marketing side of a second bar or bas mitzvah. A second bar or bas mitzvah puts religious feeling into a nice, attractive package. It's a pop-market hook, a way of luring people back to shul.

"Also, some people don't want to be prayed to. Like me, they want to pray themselves. Or, they always felt like they were on the outskirts of Jewish tradition, and they want to change that. Or, during the High Holy Days, they become irritated by their Jewish illiteracy, hearing the music and not knowing the words, and feeling like a stranger in the shul. Nobody likes to feel left out in the cold. Others may be seeking spiritual tools for brooding about life in a deeper context. More than anything else, I was reaffirming my Judaism and my membership in the Jewish community. However, I was also trying to return to my boyhood. To my innocence. To my relative innocence, if you will."

"So did you find it?" asked Dick.

"In some ways, yes. A little bearded man, with pudgy fingers and doubtful personal hygiene, taught several of us boys Hebrew. We were restless. We kept kidding around. He would threaten to report us to our parents, tell them we were wasting their money. We learned: this is how you pronounce these symbols as you read backwards. This is how you chant in your nose. The big thing was, not only to get up there in the shul, in front of everybody, and carry the Torah, and read from it, but to read your speech in Hebrew, and then in English. God forbid you should drop the Torah. We were told it would be a terrible sin.

"The surprising thing for me is, that I also want to go beyond my boyhood. To touch my childhood memories. But there I run into amnesia. Or tantalizing hints. Once upon a time, long ago, pleasant little memories used to come back to me. And then they stopped. I keep thinking that maybe if I visit the Bessarabian town of my early childhood, Akkerman, now called Belgorod-Dniestrovski, on the western shore of the Dniester estuary, near Odessa, something important may happen to me."

Sid pointed to a spot on his right forehead, just above the outer corner of his eyebrow.

"There's a bit of glass buried here," he said. "When I was a child in this ancient town, I was carrying a glass of milk. And I crossed a freshly waxed floor and slipped and fell. The glass shattered, and some slivers went into my forehead. About fifteen years ago a couple came out by themselves. But there's still a piece I can feel. Sometimes I absently finger the scar, and suddenly I remember that I can't remember, and that saddens me. We all have childhood amnesia, but for me those early years are especially hidden, maybe because they exist in a language I once knew but have long forgotten—Russian. Doris and I are going to the Soviet Union next week. First Helsinki. Then Moscow, Kharkov, Kiev, and so on.

"Anyhow, my father's father was a shammes. He carried out some of the ceremonies of the temple. I didn't know him too well. I sort of knew him for a few moments, you might say. He was never a member of the temple. He was not that observant, because he had to work. He was in ladies' garments, and they were open on Saturdays. He used to go to temple on the High Holy Days, and that, as I recall, is about all he ever did. I went more than he did. But not because I was more observant or more attached to religion. Again, I felt more attached culturally. But even before that, when we lived in Manhattan, I used to go to service. But I would go like my father. Which is to say, I would fast most of the time on Yom Kippur. And that was about it. I went to Hebrew school for five years. I began when I was eight. And I was a good student. The last two years, we spoke nothing but Hebrew in the class. And to this day I understand more of the prayers than probably ninety-eight percent of the people who walk into a shul."

"Old buddy, how do you feel about cremation?" Dick asked suddenly.

Sid was startled. "Cremation?"

"Cremation."

"For myself? Good Jews don't believe in it."

"Why not?"

"It's a very old taboo. Nowadays there's another good reason. Who wants to be reminded of German crematoriums? Why do you ask?"

"Nora's going to be cremated. But I'll beat her to it. By a mile."

With that, Dick, closing his eyes, fell silent.

After a long, heavy pause, Doris said to Sid, "Up until the time you were five years old you spoke nothing but Yiddish."

"No, up till the time I was five and a half. At twelve I was vice-president of the junior congregation. Part of my job as vice-president was to conduct Sabbath services. So I knew something about these things. But the guy who put me off, and put me down, was my mother's father. He came over from Russia when I was eleven. And he lived in the same house with us. I used to lay tefillin, morning and night. And I was a bit of a precocious student. At sixteen I was already a sophomore at college. I was at home one night, doing some homework. And my mother's father walks in. It's Succoth. And he comes home from shul all full of enthusiasm for this holiday. And he says to me in Yiddish, 'You weren't at the service tonight. Let's go through the ceremony now.' I said in Yiddish, 'What I'm doing is pretty complicated. Give me a little time. I want to finish this off.' So he goes to his room. And he comes back and says impatiently, 'Are you ready now?' I said, 'No, I still need a little more time.' And he shouts something I've never forgotten. 'You're a Goy!' I said, 'Me? The guy who does all these things? Who goes to shul on Shabbes and does the tefillin?' I was furious. I said to my mom, 'I'll never talk to this man again! This man is insane! He has completely lost his perspective about what's going on here! *I* of all people!' When I was first bar mitzvahed I wrote my bar mitzvah speeches myself. I was good at it. And he was proud of me then. And he had to go and piss on the parade, to put it bluntly. I never spoke to him after that. And I went to shul only infrequently. And I stopped laying tefillin. He died about a year later."

"Did you discuss with Doris your desire to have a bar mitzvah?" asked Nora.

"I was concerned for only one reason," said Doris. "Sid was determined to do everything to perfection. But he doesn't have a singing voice. So I thought, 'How's he going to do this? Oh my God, should I tell him? Maybe he should drop it.'"

"I would blow one melody after another," Sid said. "Up until three weeks before, I didn't know if I'd be able to pull it off. I'm not the kind of guy to go up there and bluff. I had to know that every note was right."

"He was working so hard," said Doris. "He had tapes of himself that he was listening to all the time—in the bathroom, in the car, wherever we went. I thought, 'My God, *I'm* going to memorize this if he doesn't stop!' But I was all for him. I thought, 'This is my bar mitzvah boy!'"

"A couple of times while I was preparing," said Sid, "I told the cantor, 'I don't know if I'm going to make this.' He said, 'You're going to do fine.' As it went on, my excitement increased. And I had this great feeling of 'Hey! I'm doing it!' When it was all over, I hugged the cantor. This guy had encouraged me. He was unbelievable. His mild manner, his teaching ability, his knowledge, but above all his beautiful voice, made working with him a real pleasure."

"Everything turned out just great that day," Doris said. "My mom had to come from New Jersey. She had been ill. So for her to make the trip, we hired somebody to drive her to Port Washington."

"I said to her mom, 'Look, it's a long trip,'" said Sid. "'You're not all that well. Don't overdo. In order to get there by 10:00, you have to leave about 8:00. Which means you have to get up at 6:00.'"

"I was so beside myself," said Doris. "I actually got in my car and drove over the George Washington Bridge, so on the way back I could say, 'Well, you're approaching Exit So-and-so, and you have three more to go, and then take a right.' I made a tape of the thing."

"Her mom almost drove us nuts," said Sid. "We gave this guy the directions. And I said, 'Don't worry about it. He's going to *be* there. He's going to make it on time.' But her mom said, 'He won't know. He's a New Jersey boy.' She was giving us this negative stuff."

"Arrangements," said Doris. "Seeing that mom would *be* there. I felt she was representative of the family, so I wanted her to *be* there. When Sid presented me to his family, he felt that I was of a Christian faith. Because in the Jewish religion, if your mom is Christian you're not a Jew. My name was Rothman. And my great-grandfather was a rabbi. But that didn't matter. Sid's mom, as a good Jewish woman, took to her bed when he told her he was going to marry a shiksa."

"Figuratively," said Sid.

"So how many people were at the bar mitzvah?" asked Nora.

"At the luncheon about eighty-five," replied Sid. "Everybody I knew was there—except you two, unfortunately. And everybody was so warm, happy. We had the whole restaurant to ourselves. He put a sign on the door—CLOSED. He did a very fine job. I mean, this was not just. Not that I'm trying to in any way be grandiose about it. This was not just some little luncheonette type of operation."

"So what was the low point?" asked Nora.

"Are you going to tell the truth?" Doris asked Sid with a mysterious smile.

"Of course," said Sid, looking embarrassed. "She could just as well have passed it by, and I probably wouldn't have mentioned it. But since she said it. . . . It's something involving her. She told you all about her mom. Well, after everybody sings Happy Birthday, I get up and say a few words. And my daughter says a few words. And then Doris gets up, and she says, 'I want you to know that I'm very happy you all came here and had an opportunity to meet my mom.' I said, 'My goodness. This is my party and she's talking about her mom again.'"

"Sid was so disappointed in me for having said what I did. Oh, you were. You were hurt."

"So what did you wear for your second bar mitzvah?" asked Nora.

"Everything, down to my underwear and socks, was brand-new," Sid replied. "I felt like a virgin."

"He was a doll," said Doris. "My bar mitzvah boy."

"I did one little thing which was my own innovation," said Sid. "I said, 'Rabbi. I want to say one little blessing that I want to add to the ceremony. It has nothing to do with the formality of the ceremony.' And I told him what it was. And he said, 'By all means.' So after the business was over, I said something in Hebrew, which comes in many prayers. 'Blessed art Thou, oh Lord, who has sanctified us, and glorified us, and brought us to this happy occasion.' I think that if anything captures my feelings about my second bar mitzvah, it's the fact that I wanted to say that."

"Sid, the Met's going to have a great Florentine Renaissance drawings exhibition," said Dick suddenly. "With a couple by Leonardo. I know how much you admire his drawings. I remember your saying, about a study of drapery he did in his early twenties,

'What distinguishes it from other master drawings is that there's so much love in it.'"

"Though he's stricken with a probably fatal illness," Sid thought, "he's vitally interested in a master drawings exhibition, which he may not live to see."

"Thanks for telling me," he said.

Leaning forward tensely, hoping to hear a revelation from the country of the deathly ill, a revelation he hoped would be of great use to him, for he sensed he himself was heading with increasing speed toward that dark country, he asked, "Dick, is there something you'd like to share with me?"

"You know my situation, don't you?"

"No."

"The cancer has spread."

No one had clarified this for him, so Sid felt he had been unfairly left out. He wanted to cry about Dick Gallagher's terrible condition.

Sounds of a cat war in the garden. Throwing off the blanket with startling agility, Dick strode rapidly to the French doors, vigorously opened one and clapped his hands forcefully. The cat sounds stopped.

"How sudden, lithe, youthful his movements are," Sid marveled. "How desperately sick *is* he?"

Still standing, and frowning, Dick said to the Sid Littles, "Nora doesn't know whose side she's on. She became a porno queen. But I don't hold that against her. [Unintelligible] She slept with fifty men in one night, but that's her right. [Unintelligible] Phone the Plaza Hotel," he ordered Sid. "Say you're calling for Dick Gallagher. Insist on being heard. No more than five minutes. Do it right now! [Unintelligible] Life isn't worth living this way. And the longer is too little. [Unintelligible] I'm going to press the case for murder against this son of a bitch. [Unintelligible]"

"Darling, please sit down. You're very tired," said Nora.

"Yes. I'm very tired," said Dick meekly, obeying, reminding Sid of Dick's sudden switch from hostility to sweetness back in Union Hospital.

As the Littles, sensing it was time to leave, stood up, Dick said apologetically, "I hope there'll be some improvement next time you come."

"I hope so too!" said Sid fervently, hugging him.

At the door, out of earshot of Dick, who had gone to the bathroom, but in Doris's presence, Nora, staring at Sid, asked, "Will you please write the *Times* obit? Do it for me, if not for poor Richard."

"Nora, please!" cried Sid, opening his eyes wide, and once again remembering her thrusting her manicured long fingers into his mouth. He was surprised and embarrassed by the intensity of his response.

Doris looked startled.

"He looks terrible. Awful. Frightening," she said on Confederate Street.

"He won't last long," said Sid heavily.

"What was that about an obit?" she asked.

Sid explained.

"Where's the harm?" she asked. "Why not write one for poor Richard?"

"Because poor Richard's still alive. And because I'm not a fucking obit writer."

Since Sid rarely used such four-letter words, Doris was shocked into silence. The Littles proceeded to the garage containing their new, white Lexus.

TWO

Helsinki . . . Moscow . . . Kharkov. . . . It was mid-May, and Sid and Doris were on a whirlwind group tour. Thirty-two Americans in all. In Kharkov a change of schedule: the group would proceed to ancient Kiev, capital of the Ukraine, not by air, as scheduled, but by express night train. A climbing of high railroad-car steps. Lurching of hot American bodies. Mess of luggage blocking the corridor. The cars of the noisy electric train swaying.

Two young Russian women brought everybody a glass of hot tea in a filigreed metal holder. One of them said hot tea cooled you off. Sid remembered his mother saying the same thing. Sipping the tea, he grew hotter, but it was pleasant holding the glass. The samovar was at the car's forward end, opposite the unisex toilet. Good to know where you could pee, because a senior bladder could catch you like a seizure. Both the corridor and the compartments sported red gingham window curtains. Somebody lowered a couple of corridor windows, causing powerful hot drafts that tore at the curtains.

Sid glanced occasionally at the flat Ukraine land, which reminded him of Kansas. Night fell slowly. He and Doris slept in their underwear, she in the lower berth. The express turned out to be a milk train, making many night stops, some lengthy. Clanging of heavy metal. Loud, rough Russian voices. Wild female laughter somewhere in the car.

He dreamed he was in a suite at the Plaza Hotel, and poor Dick was sitting on the left, smiling pathetically while Nora, the porno queen who had slept with fifty men, was making eye advances to Sid. Sid responded by embracing her. Then Sid and Nora went into a mushy, wet kiss. Then Sid had two fingers in Nora's moist vagina. As he removed his fingers, out of her vagina slowly emerged an erect, circumcised penis. Stroking it, he heard a man's single groan, followed by silence. He stroked faster, faster. The penis ejaculated, the fluid continuing for longer than he had expected. Surprised and envious regarding the volume of semen (the years had taken their toll; he himself was no longer capable of a decent volume), he awoke to find himself partially erect. What in God's name was he doing having a gay dream? And why had he selected Nora, of all people, to be erotic with? Dick Gallagher's wife! The woman who had thrice thrust wet food and long, long, cold shiksa fingers into meticulous Sid's mouth! What chutzpa! "*My* ashes will be scattered over my beloved Manhattan," she had once said. Had the car's swaying brought on the dream? The old rails probably needed straightening.

The Littles' thirteenth-floor Kiev hotel room had a view of a nearby stadium and, in the distance, of a high ski jump. Exhausted by the train trip, Doris decided to sleep until lunch, whereas Sid, though he too had had a poor night, was eager to explore this mother of all Russian cities.

"If you see buildings like in Kharkov, stay close to the gutter," she said, staring at him from her single bed. They hadn't been assigned a double one.

"Sweetheart, you worry too much."

"Yes, but in Kharkov you walked too close to big buildings."

"Doris, I told you we should take a pill."

Map in hand, he strolled toward the city's center, alert to the fast traffic of cars and trolleys at the broad intersections. He knew there had been large-scale attempts to coverup anti-Semitism in this city. He had read that many Kiev Gentiles had fingered Jews for the Germans. And that the city of Kiev had wanted to pave over the notorious ravine to wipe out the memory of Babi Yar, and to build a housing project there, but that international pressure had persuaded the city not to do it. And that the Soviet Union had dragged its feet in erecting the Babi Yar monument, the plaque of which didn't even mention that Jews had been slaughtered there. And now he, a Jew who had very recently had a second bar mitzvah, and Doris, the converted Jew, were especially eager to pay their respects to the Babi Yar dead. But at the moment he was group-touring the modern city, while she was napping to recover from the effects of the phony night express.

It was a sunny day, with sharply defined shadows. Great chestnut trees in bloom. Huge upper-story concrete balconies, parts of which had fallen but had not been carted away. He had heard that immediately after the war the Russians, needing to rebuild quickly, had used watered-down cement. No doubt the true figures of people crippled or killed by falling concrete were a state secret. He remembered the cover-up of the Chernobyl nuclear power plant disaster not far from here.

Old litter and public carelessness almost everywhere. Massive, strictly functional apartment complexes in a remarkable state of disrepair. New grass struggling to sprout in soil that, although it had been roughed up, hadn't been pulverized and smoothed out. In Moscow last week the dandelions had been golden. Here and in Kharkov they had already gone to seed. Seeing people, carrying unwrapped loaves of bread, emerging from a small shop, he visited it, descending a small, slippery concrete incline and crossing a threshold of broken concrete. If he took a bad fall, whom could he sue, Mikhail Gorbachev? A long queue waiting to pay for rolls, dark bread, light bread. Great dough smells. A young female clerk deftly working an abacus.

A little later, finding himself at the enclosed Central Market, he went in. Huge spaces. Tumult of voices, noises. Bitter odors. The customers, mostly peasant-looking women, and the clerks, of both sexes, were almost all very stout. Mockery of the human figure. (And of the human spirit?) What was the Soviet life expectancy as compared with that of the States?

"In a sense I'm one of you," he thought. "I once spoke your language, which I long ago almost entirely forgot. But I'm not truly one of you, because I'm carrying American dollars in my shoulder bag, and American credit cards, and American Express travel checks, and this is the latest Leica rangefinder around my neck—black, light, sleek, expensive."

Cheap cuts of fatty beef. Large salt-pork slabs. Hog heads. Pig ears. Skinned rabbits. Pig tails. No butcher saws visible. Instead of cleavers, he saw tools suggesting battle axes out of the Middle Ages. WHACK and a large side of bone, gristle, tendon, meat was sundered. He stared at legless butcher blocks, each a cross-section of a large tree.

His mother, in America, had raved about the fruit back home in Bessarabia, saying how tasteless and odorless American fruit was by comparison. True, Kiev was in the Ukraine, not Bessarabia, but he assumed the Ukraine, with its rich black soil, also produced wonderful stuff. But where was it? He saw only greenish, wizened cherries; reddish, shriveled apples; pathetic, wrinkled oranges; wrinkled grapes; measly strawberries. No bananas, pineapples, grapefruit. Why couldn't he smell the many roses, carnations and irises for sale?

He absently felt the ancient forehead scar above his right eyebrow, with the sliver of glass still encased in it, and recalled Nora saying, "It's as if you have a horn sprouting there!" He guiltily remembered Dick's frightening condition.

"What am I doing here, in Kiev, having fun after having fun in Helsinki and Moscow?" he thought. "But I have a right to enjoy myself while I still can. Because who knows the meaning of this ominous feeling I often have these days?"

He went to a powerful boulevard nearby and observed people strolling under massive chestnut trees whose clustered flowers suggested fat, tawny, pyramidal candles.

"Excuse me, sir. Speak English?" a pretty woman in her twenties asked him with an American accent. Her figure was muscular.

The extraordinary thing was, she reminded him of Nora. Or a young version of Nora. Same blond hair, blue eyes. Same height. Same cool Scandinavian Protestant look. But instead of feeling guilty toward Dick, or toward Doris, for that matter, he experienced again the pleasurable sensations of the dream, a surging of youthfulness.

"Yes."

"Know where the main post office is?"

"No."

"It's supposed to be around here somewhere. Isn't Kiev wonderful?" she cried, gesturing. "Have you seen the monastery and the catacombs?"

She had a strong, low, self-confident voice, again like Nora's. But whereas Nora liked to wear designer clothes, this young lady wore blue jeans, and a blue denim jacket with anodized metal buttons, and a blue leather shoulder bag, and blue topsiders.

"The Blue Girl," he thought, remembering Gainsborough's courtly, exquisitely dressed, almost too beautiful Blue Boy, with the great feathered hat in his right hand.

"Not yet. Where are you from?"

"San Francisco. You come down from Moscow?"

"Kharkov."

"Is Kharkov worth seeing?"

Her eyes were very blue. Her mouth was surrounded by fine wrinkles. Her blond hair was shoulder-length, with ashen streaks. Each of her strong hands wore two or three rings, some gold, some silver. Aquamarine, turquoise. He detected a subtle odor of perfume.

"Yes. There's a huge square. But if you go, I suggest you don't walk close to buildings. Many have concrete balconies or parapets that have rotted. Sizable chunks have fallen."

"Thanks for the warning. So long," she said, and was soon lost in the crowd.

At some fountains with a number of small geysers spraying the area with a fine mist (people were dining nearby under blue awnings), he was approached by a tall street photographer wearing a conical black hat and carrying a well-used Nikon. The man advertised his services with placards attached to a tall aluminum tripod.

"Fine camera!" the man said, smiling and pointing at Sid's camera. "Name?"

"Leica."

"Ah! Layka! Layka!"

"Leica. Leica. Like like her."

"Yes! Layka! Layka! Very expensive!" said the man, grinning while reaching out a broad hand to indicate he wanted to examine the camera.

Sid unslung and handed it to him.

"You sell this me for rubles?" asked the man, returning the Leica.

Sid laughed and said, "No thanks."

Pointing to the fool's gold stone on Sid's left ring finger, the man asked, "This?"

"Fool's gold. Pyrite." The man stared at it. The man wasn't getting it, so Sid added, "Too difficult to explain."

"You like my Kiev?" the man asked.

"Yes. But some of your buildings have been falling down."

The man laughed. "Very safe! No kill Americans! Only Russians!"

"And Chernobyl? How many Russians were killed there?" asked Sid. "Your government won't say."

The man shrugged.

"Big tragic," he said, and presented Sid with a business card, on the back of which was printed **FINESTG PHOTOGRAPHIC IN FINET FRENCH STYEL**.

"Here you are again!" said the Blue Girl with the blond hair, walking up to Sid and smiling broadly, revealing strong teeth.

"Hello! Did you find the post office?"

"Your daughter?" asked the photographer.

"Yes," said Sid.

"It's just down the street," said the Blue Girl.

There was a woman selling flowers near the curb. The Blue Girl bought a bunch of irises.

"For you, Dad," she said, handing it to him with a smile.

"*Thank you*," he said, surprised and moved. "You won't believe it, but purple irises are my favorite flower. Their odor has haunted me since my childhood."

"Maybe I knew that. Maybe we knew each other in another life." She laughed.

"I accept that—metaphorically," he said.

"I'm Brigid."

"I'm Sid."

They shook hands. In a moment or two they parted again. Smiling, and carrying the irises, which he occasionally smelled, he continued his walk under the chestnut trees.

"Brigid, the Blue Girl. Sweet spirit," he thought, remembering the pleasure of last night's dream.

Suddenly he saw himself as a child, as little Sidney in Bessarabia, long ago. Little Sidney in Bessarabia loved irises, especially purple ones. His heart jumped when he saw them. They reminded him of summer, a cottage, and of a blond little girl in blue. He was riding in a carriage on a dirt road, listening to the clopclop of hooves, thinking of a fairy tale about geese and two lost girls. There wasn't a speck in the sky. The road curved, cooking in the sun. The fields were flat to the horizon. A farm. A searing barn. Hay smells. Geese racing at him, honking, eyes glaring, bills hissing, necks and heads outstretched like clubs. Screaming, he ran. They fascinated him, but if they kept scaring him he'd ask his dad to beat them. Then they too would know what it was like to be small, innocent, frightened. The day cooled. Evening. Fields. Horses. Driver. Sky. Another dirt road. Stones. High grass. Hedges. A cottage among birches. Behind it a garden with purple irises making him heady with their smell and color. And, standing among them, the little blue girl.

Again he saw himself as a child, and Aunt Jennie, fifteen, one of his dad's two sisters, was giving him a silver ring, saying she had something to show him. So while the grownups were talking in the kitchen he followed her to her room, where she bolted the door, stretched out on the bed, lifted her skirt, pulled down her drawers, pulled out his penis and arranged him on top of her. She said it was an important part of this game to tell no one about it. It was a game he hadn't played before. They returned to the kitchen, she looking innocent, he feeling smug with his large secret.

It was morning, time for little Sidney to get up and play.

"Stand up so I can dress you," said his Nana.

Standing, he stared at her bosom, which seemed to be stuffed with feathers.

"What are you looking at?" she muttered. "Foo! Filthy mind!"

"I'm not."

"I can hear you thinking. Stand still."

"I don't want you to dress me."

"It doesn't matter what you don't want," she said coarsely, in a peasant voice.

"I'm a grownup. You mustn't look at me when I'm not dressed."

His Nana laughed.

"And you think this is grownup?" she asked, tapping his penis with a forefinger.

"Don't!"

"Who wiped and washed you all these years? And hugged and kissed you when your mom and dad were away and you were lonely? And let you crawl into her bed when you were afraid of the bogeyman? Who spoke up for you when your dad was angry? So what do you have to hide from your Nana? Nothing! Understand? You, a little worm, speaking to your Nana like that!"

"I don't want you to dress me."

"Oh? So we'll dress ourself this morning? All right, go ahead."

He struggled with his clothes. It was hard work.

"Terrific!" his Nana cried, and pulled him by the wrist into the living room, where his mom was sewing.

"Today our grownup insisted on dressing himself," said his Nana.

Sidney's mom stared, then laughed until tears came.

His Nana led him back to his room, where she undressed him. He covered his penis with his hands.

"You're not going to see it!" he cried.

"Oh? Maybe you want to see me, is that it? All right!"

She opened her blouse and spilled out white balloons with cherries in the center. He stared.

"Here, touch them," she said, and put his hand on a cherry.

He pulled it back as if burned. She laughed, then dumped the balloons inside her blouse.

"I suppose you'd like to touch me somewhere else too," she said, and laughed again.

She fingered his penis.

"Foo," she said softly. "A little nothing. Well, are we going to have more trouble about dressing?"

"No," he whispered.

She dressed him. So many things to think about with a head full of sawdust.

Suddenly two lost Russian words came back with great pleasure to Sid Little in Kiev: karandash (pencil) and khleb (bread).

"What a marvel the human brain is," he thought, inhaling the irises' aroma. "What I believed was lost to me, now comes back effortlessly, almost against my will."

He returned to his hotel, where he borrowed a blue glass vase at the desk, brought it up to his room and stood the irises in it. Doris was still asleep. Sleepy himself now, he napped in the adjoining bed. Again he dreamed of Nora, but this time it wasn't foreplay. Still dressed, she had removed her panties and was underneath him and guiding his penis, saying "Slowly, slowly," as if he might hurt her. But then it turned out she wasn't Nora after all, but the Blue Girl, and he was pleased and confused and embarrassed.

When he and Doris were washing up and dressing for the group dinner downstairs, he told her how the Nora look-alike had given the irises to him.

"She's a nut. Very neurotic," said Doris sharply, surprising him. "Who needs flowers when we're racing from city to city."

"She's a very nice young lady," he responded defensively. "She did me a great service."

He explained how the irises had brought back some of his lost childhood memories, and how grateful he was to have them, and how he sensed more would soon come.

"Oh. Good!" she said. "That's wonderful, Sidney. In that case, I like her."

At dinner Sid and Doris shared a table with a softspoken man named Freddy and his wife Olive. Retired, Freddy had been in ladies' garments. About a dozen years ago he had had a stroke, as a consequence of which the left side of his mouth suggested a Mona Lisa smile, and his left eye, larger than its mate, glistened as if with an overload of tears. Olive was stocky, with a broad face, olive skin and thick gray hair. The meat was cold and extremely tough, the fries soggy, the potato pancakes leaden. Sid downed two tumblers of a tart, bitter juice the waiter called pomegranate.

"We were assured this is a first-class hotel," said Freddy. "They forgot to tell the food that."

After dinner, in the beriozka bar (rubles were unacceptable; only hard currency would do), where the four tourists had soft drinks together, Sid told about his visit to the Central Market, about his walk under the chestnut trees on the great boulevard, and about his very pleasant experience with a young San Francisco woman, dressed all in blue.

In the morning the group toured Kiev by private bus, then visited the Monastery of the Caves, founded in 1051 and situated on a height. The freshly gilded domes were easy to look at against the cloudless blue sky. Views of a river and of a distant, long bridge. Sid had the sense, inside the monastery's walls, that it had once been a self-contained village. Ludmilla, the group's local Intourist guide, a husky young woman with a boyish bob, who wore a loosely flowing gray dress that reached down to her powerful calves, said that in the old days a large monastery like this might have owned several hundred thousand acres and ten thousand serfs.

The group went down steep, slippery, cobbled streets to reach the catacombs, where a diorama showed a Stone Age family and some spearheads and arrowheads. Walking uphill beside Doris near a church, and smelling mown hay that lay in masses beyond a wrought-iron fence, Sid was reminded of similar odors in his childhood. Suddenly several Russian words came back to him: zhaupa (backside), Ya khotu pukatch (I want to move my bowels), and porokhot (steamship). And then, instantaneously, he recovered several childhood memories. A hot, still day in little Sidney's Bessarabian courtyard. Smoke from three wood fires lingering in the air. Above each fire bubbled a cauldron of plum jam viciously, scurvily, bitterly—black, purple, with violet scum that was scooped up with wooden spatulas and cast into wooden buckets. Smelling the jam odors, he stared at the smoke, at the two maids in their peasant skirts, and at his mom supervising everything, and remembered the little blond girl in blue.

"Mom, I'm going for a walk," he said on the ship heading from France toward America.

"Don't get lost."

"I can't get lost on a ship. There are corridors."

"Oh? We'll see."

He wandered here and there. It was all so simple. But when he tried to return to his cabin he found that everything was mixed up. He started to cry. A young steward led him to his mom. How shameful that he, a Russian child going to the land of gold, was crying on a jolly ship named *La Lorraine*.

"Fine little boy," said the Bessarabian barber.

Holding his dad's hand, Sidney felt proud on the narrow street. True, he had cried while in the barber's chair, but he must have made up for it, because his dad hadn't referred to it.

"I guess I behaved fine just by being who I am, a great little man," thought Sidney.

Playing in his courtyard, he saw his dad in his dad's study, a cool, airy room off the yard, with a large door and a large window. His dad, sitting at his desk, looked dignified and solemn as he worked methodically on his papers, pen in hand. Sidney was seized by an uncontrollable impulse. He ran into the study, shouted "Dad!" and waited until his dad looked up, then thrust his behind up at him. Now he was frightened, because his dad was a grim, determined man, conscious of his dignity and insistent on receiving the respect he believed due him. His dad rose from his chair and slowly, grimly pursued Sidney into the yard. Sidney darted here, there, shouting, "I'm sorry! I'm sorry! I didn't mean it!" There was no escape. His dad followed him implacably, never hurrying. His dad cornered him, spanked him and, still silent, returned to his desk. Sidney observed him tearfully, the solemn man who was as methodical in administering punishment as in making notations on his mysterious papers.

Sid Little, in Kiev, felt flushed with pleasure as he tasted these memories, as if he had drunk a fine old wine. Fearing he might spook other childhood memories that had lain dormant for decades, he decided to keep his quest's success private for a while.

After lunch the group visited St. Sophia Cathedral, founded in 1037. More freshly gilded domes. But the serene blue sky was giving way to glowering clouds. Ludmilla said that now they would visit the Babi Yar ravine. Sid—thinking, "In the rain?"—imagined a wet raw ravine backed by woods.

"Babi Yar was rehearsal of German practice of genocide," said Ludmilla in the bus. "Nazis murder many Jews there. Also many, many Kiev people. Landslide fill original ravine. New ravine made by machine."

She said that in September 1941 the Germans had machine-gunned fifty thousand to seventy thousand people there, mostly Jews. That for the next two years the Syrets death camp was located there. And that when the Germans retreated in August and September of 1943 they destroyed the camp and dug up thousands of bodies, which they burned in large ovens, scattering the ashes in the ravine's vicinity.

A heavy rain began as the group were being driven toward Babi Yar, and Ludmilla said Babi Yar was therefore cancelled as part of the Kiev tour. The Americans returned to their hotel, the half-dozen Jews among them disconcerted because they hadn't been able to pay their respects in person to the murdered Jews.

"Should we go back on our own?" Sid asked Doris in their room. "It depresses me not to have been there."

"Go in the morning?"

"Good idea."

But though Sid was depressed, the aroma of the purple irises, and their great beauty, and their ability to remind him vividly of the Blue Girl, the Nora look-alike, comforted him, and aroused a feeling almost like love, which was strange inasmuch as he barely knew her. Bending over them carefully, he inhaled the scent deeply several times, savoring it.

"I'm taking these to Odessa," he announced.

"That's crazy."

"Not for me it isn't."

"Why schlepp them?"

"Because they bring back memories precious to me."

"What memories?"

"Of my childhood."

"Why haven't you told me?"

"I did. I need not to share them for a while. Okay?"

"The others will think you're weird."

"Good. I've reached the time of life where I want people to see me as I really am."

She sighed.

After dinner he said to Doris and the Browns in the beriozka bar (Brown was Freddy's and Olive's surname), "I probably wanted to see Babi Yar more than anything else in this town. It's very frustrating. Our guide, Ludmilla, said the original ravine got filled in by a landslide. Convenient landslide when you're willing to cover up what happened."

"Be fair," said Doris. "She gave us lots of details. What do you expect? This is her country. She's a patriot."

"All right, I take it back. I'm glad religion is making a comeback in the Soviet Union, but frankly, I've had it up to here with gilded cupolas. For a country that's broke, why are they spending so much on gold leaf?"

The rain became a downpour during the night and lasted until noon. It was so heavy that the morning tour of Kiev was also cancelled, which didn't disappoint the tourists, for they were tired of climbing in and out of buses and craning to stare at cupolas. The Littles reluctantly abandoned the idea of going to Babi Yar.

In the afternoon, heading for Odessa, the Americans were bused to the Kiev airport, where, in a large, dingy lobby, they tried to eat the box lunch the first-class hotel had prepared for them. It included slices of salami, three-quarters of which were white globules of fat, and heavy slices of smoked salmon that was extremely salty and that smelled very fishy. The Littles settled for some dark bread, a small tomato each, a chunk of cucumber, and bottled orange Fanta. Sid had placed the irises, which he had wrapped in a moist Kiev newspaper, on the chair beside him. He occasionally glanced solicitously at them. None of the other members of the group seemed to notice them. Freddy, with the Mona Lisa smile, reported that the men's room was like the one at the chief beriozka in Moscow (foreign-exchange gift shop): a horror; and reminded them (as if they needed reminding) that there had been pervasive urine smells even in the Kremlin.

The flight was supposed to leave at 2:00 but Mischa, the Intourist guide who accompanied the group on the entire tour, said it would be delayed until 3:15 because of "a side wind" in Odessa, so some people napped. The four single women, all from southern California and all middle-aged, were in the ladies' room when Mischa suddenly announced that the Aeroflot plane was in a great hurry to take off. He and Michael, the young, tall, handsome, drawling tour director from Kentucky, promptly strode down a stairway and out a door, followed by the group, with the exception of Doris and the four ladies.

Doris ran into the ladies' room to warn the latter. The four ladies emerged scurrying and looking very angry. Catching up, one of them screamed "You're incompetent!" at Mischa. He was slight, in his mid-thirties, with good brown eyes, a straightforward manner, and shaggy brown hair that always looked uncombed. Although he was short, he had a habit of hanging his head, as if to lessen his height. Flushing, he apologized.

When the Americans entered the stand-up bus which was to take them to their plane, Sid's ears began to hurt. Seeing some Russians covering theirs, he realized that alarmingly close to the bus was an Aeroflot plane revving up its twin jets, and he covered his own, Doris following suit. As the plane moved forward slowly, the bus swung around the rear of it. A short-haired white dog ran onto the tarmac. "Soviet insanity," Sid remarked to her.

Aside from three male Russian passengers, the Americans were the only ones on the plane. The stewardess, who wore bright pink lipstick and a dark brown uniform, served seltzer water in brown ceramic cups without handles. Most of the passengers, including Doris, slept during the flight, but Sid kept watching the flat land, which contained many farms. As the plane neared Odessa it flew over the Dniester estuary. He glimpsed gleaming wetlands. "Akkerman, in Bessarabia, is nearby, where I spent much of my childhood," he thought. "Will Doris and I be allowed to go there? Will it really happen that I'll visit it after all those years?"

The plane swung out over the Black Sea before landing. And there it was: Odessa, Paris of the Black Sea, with its famous Potemkin Steps and beautiful opera house. Birthplace of famous Jewish violinists, Jewish writers, and of Sid Little of America. His heart pounded uncomfortably in excitement as the plane touched down.

At the airport to greet the Littles was a stout woman in dark clothes, holding three long-stem purple irises wrapped in a cellophane that crackled angrily whenever she moved it. This was Helen, sister-in-law of a second cousin of Sid's, who had learned of their coming and who, as a relation, had insisted on meeting them. Seeing the purple irises Sid was carrying, she looked surprised, forestalled. She handed her irises to him.

"Strange coincidence," he thought uncomfortably. "An ominous sign for me? She's no Helen of Troy."

In her sixties, a widow, retired as a pediatrician (or a gynecologist; the Littles weren't able to get it straight), and currently working as a chemist (or pharmacist), she was tall and very generously built. Her face under a thatch of wild, dyed henna hair was somber, her flaring nostrils cavernous. She hugged and mouth-kissed the Littles. Doris had corresponded with her, writing in English and receiving replies in Russian, and had assured Sid that Helen would bring an interpreter. But Helen hadn't, so the Littles had a communication problem inasmuch as they knew no Russian, and Helen knew only a smattering of English and Yiddish. They tried to enlist Mischa's help but Mischa at the moment was too busy. Given the paucity of linguistic means, it was exhausting for the Littles to try to communicate with her. Much of their conversation consisted of a waving of arms, a twisting of torsos, a twitching of fingers, and facial expressions Sid thought might have been put to more lucrative use in a minstrel show. But Helen somehow managed to inform Doris that she had taken three days off from work to spend time with the Littles, so Doris invited her to have dinner with the group this evening, a gesture Helen promptly accepted.

The Americans, together with Helen, Mischa and Kentucky Michael, proceeded by Intourist bus toward the Black Sea Hotel in Odessa's harbor district, Sid holding the irises carefully, almost tenderly, like a chalice. Mischa warned the group that, unlike other Soviet cities (inland cities) they had visited, Odessa was a port, consequently the crime rate was a good deal higher here.

"Don't walk alone or in the evening. And watch out for pickpockets," he said.

"Then why are we staying in the harbor district?" asked Freddy.

"I don't know," replied Mischa. "It wasn't my decision. But I assure you it's okay."

"From whose point of view?" asked Freddy.

Mischa shrugged, smiling in embarrassment.

Seeing very old, cobbled streets, and very old, solid buildings, and glimpsing through archways old, disordered, cobbled courtyards with children and dogs playing happily in them, Sid thought, "I was born here. Mom and Dad may have known these very streets. What part of town was I born in? Was I born at home or in a hospital?"

A sandhill tufted with fierce seagrass. Great rotten marshes. Steaming sea air. Bottle flies. Gulls circling high. Why was little Sidney staring, empty-headed? Didn't he know he couldn't think while his eyes were being held as if by wires running to the marshes and grass? He dug a hole in the sand and buried a little wooden boat his Uncle Volodya had carved for him. Later, he couldn't find it. When he told his mom about it, she told his dad. They laughed.

"What's so funny?" thought Sidney. "It could happen even to a grownup."

A strong wind blew up. Tents flew. The sea churned white. Men cried hoarsely. Children were silent. A commotion in the sea. Men dashed in, swam frantically. A man rowed madly. They shoved a young man into the boat and brought him ashore. One drowned here only last month.

A gangplank smelling of tar and rotten fish. A sailboat on the estuary. The man with the silver mustache, hard blue eyes and furrowed brown forehead shoved off. A gust sent Sidney's sailor cap flying into the water. The boat turned back to retrieve it but the cap was gone. Forever. The sea. A boat. A cap. The facts were plain, yet no one could solve Sidney's problem.

"No," said Dad firmly. "Naked is how you must be. Just like the other kids."

Dad began to remove Sidney's bathing shorts. Sidney writhed.

"Stop it! Stop being ashamed of what God gave you."

"Why don't the grownups go naked then?"

"Because they're grownups. Hold still!"

"But the little girls will see me!" said Sidney, pointing to the naked children playing at the water's edge.

"They're not ashamed. What's so special about you?"

Grownup hands gripped him. He cried. But Dad knew better than to be persuaded by a child. Sidney stood naked on the beach, aware of the now unprotected thing between his legs.

"Run along!" said Dad.

As Sidney moved toward the water, he couldn't take his eyes off the nothings, marked by a tiny line, between the girls' legs.

As the Intourist bus neared the Black Sea Hotel, Mischa informed the group that unfortunately the hotel had been without hot water the past eight days and would probably not have any during their brief stay. Sighing and grumbling among the group. As he alighted from the bus, Sid received fleeting impressions of roughly dressed, rough-looking, unshaved men of various ages walking past the hotel entrance, and thought he could detect a moistness in the air due to the hotel's proximity to the sea.

He recalled his mother's romanticism about Odessa. She would talk about what a gay, bright city it had once been, full of culture, and would emphasize its beautiful opera house, where she had heard the great Caruso sing, and Chaliapin, the great Russian basso, sing in *Boris Godunov*. She seemed to want to imbue him with pride in having been born there, implying that Odessa had endowed him with special gifts. But what had seemed a romantic port city at a great distance now struck him as ordinary, even vaguely threatening. Which was just as well. He would save his emotions for the fabled town of his childhood, named Akkerman (White City) by the Turks in the fifteenth century (and still called Akkerman by many of its present as well as former inhabitants), and known by the Romanians as Cetatea Alba (White City), and by the Russians since 1944 as Belgorod-Dniestrovski (Beautiful City on the Dniester).

Helen waited in the lobby while the Littles went to check out their room on the fifth floor. Affording glimpses of the Black Sea, it looked out over the tops of small houses and the green of trees. It was small but clean and neat. However, there were no bath towels, so the Littles returned to the lobby, where Sid asked the female desk clerk for them.

The clerk, who wore large black earrings, laughed and said, "What for you need bath towels?"

"I don't need to explain. You should explain why there's no hot water."

The woman laughed again, earrings dancing. "Hot water? Is warm day."

"Bath. Towels."

"Bath. Towels," the woman mimicked, and laughed again, but gave the necessary order.

"Two letters for you," said Mischa, appearing from a corner of the lobby. "One for you." He handed Doris an envelope. "And one for you." He gave Sid the other.

They were from Nora Gallagher. The Littles read both. Sid's said, "Don't be heartless. Have pity. Write the obit. Love always." Doris's said, "I've asked Sid to write an obit for poor Richard. It's the decent thing. He's incredibly stubborn, or willful, whatever. Doris, please persuade him. Love."

"Christ, she hounds me halfway around the world," said Sid, groaning.

"Why are you tormenting her?" asked Doris. "Write the obit. Poor Richard."

"Poor Sidney. Give me a break. Women. It's true that you have minds different from men."

He remembered Dick's weird behavior in Union Hospital, Dick's speaking wildly, full of sound and fury, about Nora's being a porno queen who had slept with fifty men, Dick's frequent lapses into unintelligible comments, and vividly recalled how frightening Dick had looked, the terrible sea change that had come over him.

"I had a good respite for a little while, and now she's spoiled it, that Nora," he thought. Then he felt guilty. "I mustn't try to distance myself from Dick, even in my thoughts. Because at bottom we're all in this human comedy together."

"We need two vases, Doris," he said. "You ask her."

"Two?"

"I'm not going to mix my irises with Helen's."

Doris groaned. "That's crazy. Why me?"

"I asked for the bath towels, didn't I?"

"I'm not going to. You really ought to write the obit. It's the decent thing to do. I thought he was such a friend of yours."

"Forget it."

He asked the clerk if he could borrow a couple of vases. To his surprise, she readily found one for him, saying, "There's vase in your room," which reminded him that there was indeed one there, containing dusty paper roses.

Later that afternoon, in the lobby, he informed Mischa that he and Doris wanted to visit Belgorod the next day.

"You'll need the hotel manager's permission," said Mischa.

"Why? Is Belgorod off-limits?"

"No. Because you want to visit it by yourself, in addition to the group program."

"Listen, Mischa," said Sid irritably. "No hot water. A lousy hotel in the lousy harbor district. And now I need a hotel manager's permission to take a one-day trip to a nearby town that has important personal meaning for me?"

"Listen, please understand. It's out of my hands," Mischa said, smiling apologetically, adding, "You'll need an Intourist van. An Intourist driver. An Intourist interpreter. And special visas."

"Special visas?"

"Because your current visas don't include an extra town."

"Soviet robbery," said Doris.

The Littles went to the hotel manager's office, where Mischa interpreted for Sid. The manager, a buxom middle-aged woman with a prominent gold tooth, asked Sid why he wanted to visit Belgorod.

"To see a first cousin," replied Sid.

Heavy phoning by the manager, followed by a conversation in Russian between her and Mischa, after which Mischa told Sid, "The trip is possible but it will be very expensive."

"How expensive?"

Mischa calculated in pencil on a loose sheet of paper. "Three hundred and twenty-five dollars."

"Highway robbery," said Doris angrily.

"We'll do it," Sid said.

About an hour later, when the Littles noticed that Freddy and Olive weren't in the lobby before dinner, waiting to go into the dining room, they asked Michael, the Kentucky tour director, about them and learned that Freddy had been mugged near the hotel and was still up in his room with Olive. Just then Freddy and Olive appeared. Freddy looked pale and shaky, and his drooping left eye glistened.

"What happened?" asked Sid, concerned.

"I needed to stretch my legs," replied Freddy quietly, "so I walked around the block. Two big guys, smelling of alcohol, are walking behind me. One of them grabs me from behind and pins my arms. The other goes through my pockets, takes my money and my old Omega Seamaster watch, which I bought in Mexico City. They shoved me and ran away."

"Terrible," said Sid, making a face. "How do you feel?"

"Fine."

"He's not fine," said Olive. "They knocked him down. He could have broken his hip. Or a knee, or something."

"I'm fine," said Freddy. "The fall didn't even break my glasses."

"The guy gets mugged and says he's fine," said Sid.

"Oh Freddy, I'm so glad you're okay," Doris said.

"I warned him not to go out by himself," said Olive. "I wanted to go with him, but I needed to wash my hair—in cold water. Eight days they've been without hot water. Who needs this? I'll be so glad to get back to the States. He doesn't listen. He never takes my advice."

"Wrong," said Freddy.

"Wonder what's for dinner," said Olive. "Maybe, by mistake, something decent."

Near little Sidney's courtyard was an abandoned small house with stairs leading down to a cellar door off the street. Sometimes, observing the stairs, he wondered what was behind the door. One hot day he found a cat down there, coughing, vomiting, shivering. He had nothing against that cat. Nevertheless something caused him to throw a rock at it, which hit its side. He expected the cat to jump in pain and run away. Instead, the cat winced, and glanced at him with a half-open mouth, mustache twitching. "I'm probably dying," he imagined the cat saying, "so you're right to stone me." Leaving, he told himself never to let anyone know he threw the stone.

He and his mom were walking home from the market. Across the street was a jail beyond a cobbled yard. An unseen woman screamed. A peasant woman in a heavy skirt ran crying out of the yard and up the street. Two young soldiers, laughing, came to the gate to watch her.

"Serves her right for trying to bring him soup," said one.

"What happened?" Sidney asked his mom.

"Nothing."

Nothing. But he had trouble forgetting it.

Night. Explosions. Everybody running down to the cellars. Later, a long evening of marching by torchlight, with men carrying signs nailed to their chests and backs.

"How can they stand the pain?" Sidney asked his mom.

Absentminded, she explained, but he didn't understand. She was worried these days, observed everything furtively. And his dad was often away. Who would have suspected that grownups would allow nails to be hammered into them? Did they cry when the nails went in?

After dinner in the Odessa hotel, in the beriozka bar on the mezzanine floor (Helen had gone home; she had been uninhibited during the meal, having wolfed at times; the food had been better than Olive had expected), Freddy, still feeling shook up, drank vodka on the rocks (Stoly, short for Stolichnaya). To keep him company, Sid drank the same. But whereas Freddy sipped his, Sid quickly knocked down a couple, then ordered a third, and even a fourth.

"What's happening?" Doris said. "Take it easy, Sid. Remember, you're no drinker."

"We're like a bunch of pilgrims in *The Canterbury Tales*," said Sid, speaking unsteadily and grinning. "We have a lonely widower. A lonely gay guy. A lonely tour director from Kentucky. Four single women huddling together. And an elderly couple having an affair. Remember how scandalized we were because they were so open about it while he was sharing a room with his wife? We felt sorry for the wife and hated him, until it turned out she isn't his wife, she's his sister. As for my so-called relative, Helen, let me say a few words about her.

"Let's take her nostrils. When I spotted her at the airport, holding the irises, with her nostrils exposed, I thought we were in Moscow, entering the metro. Her nostrils are so deep that if you look into them you can see her esophagus. And she's either a pediatrician or a gynecologist, or both, and does hemorrhoids on the side. I knew we were in deep trouble when she said, 'I've taken three days off from my job to devote them to you. I'm not leaving you. How many dollars have you brought? Do you want rubles? Are those diamonds on your fingers, or zircons? I can use lots of pancake makeup.'"

"Sid! You're drunk!" cried Doris in dismay before joining the Browns in laughter.

As he was preparing to turn in for the night, Sid noticed a spot in his fool's gold stone that looked darker and more massive than usual, and couldn't resist trying to discover what this meant. He removed from a trouser pocket a small two-bladed Swiss army knife with a red handle and, using the tip of the smaller blade, probed the dark spot. The spot promptly disintegrated into a blackish dust, horrifying him. It also angered him, so he probed further. The entire stone self-destructed into fine pieces that fell on the floor.

"Doris! Look what happened!" he said, showing her the now empty rectangular gold receptacle which had housed the stone. "An ominous portent!" he said in an agitated voice.

"Good. Now you can replace the stupid thing with a real stone."

"It could only happen to a Jew. Who else would buy a ring with fool's gold that self-destructs."

"What? You're drunk. Stop crying, for God's sake."

"It's my left eye. You know my left eye cries first."

"Oy," the woman born a half-shiksa said.

THREE

Though Helen could barely communicate with the Littles, and though the latter had been obliged to hire an Intourist interpreter for their trip to Belgorod-Dniestrovski, Helen turned up at breakfast next morning and insisted, in her role as Sidney's relative (however distant) and interpreter, on accompanying the Littles to that town. Again she carried three purple irises, which she said were for Sid's Cousin Riva in Belgorod, but once more, though reluctantly, Sid took them as an ominous sign of fate directed at him. He would have gladly left Helen behind in Odessa, but Helen was stubborn, and Doris supported her, and so early that afternoon Helen and the Littles headed westward in a pale green Intourist van.

As the van passed through Ovidiopol, a village of one-story houses, Sid thought of the trucks the Nazis had used for gassing Jews, because the van's exhaust fumes, seeping into the cabin even with all the windows open, were powerful whenever Peter, the youthful driver who spoke no English, drove under forty kilometers an hour. Sid glimpsed front-yard irises, and a doubled-over old woman sweeping the gutter with a primitive broom. He had recently read that the Roman poet Ovid had been exiled here because he had offended Emperor Augustus's moral sense by his poetry and sexual behavior.

Then, under an expansive blue sky, the Black Sea was visible on the left, and on the right were the gleaming broad arms and sinewy fingers of the Dniester estuary. Crossing the estuary via a long bridge, the van left the Ukraine and entered Bessarabia, the old bufferland between Russia, Turkey and Romania, which was currently Soviet territory. The highway, heading northward, wound among trees, vineyards and high-voltage towers, and passed a small military installation. Now came the Belgorod "new" town, showing old concrete apartment buildings that reminded Sid of Kharkov's and Kiev's rotting balconies. At last the "old" town, the fabled

Akkerman of his childhood, situated on the estuary's gleaming western shore. Deserted narrow streets. Overarching trees. Tree trunks and telephone poles whitewashed to the height of a tall man's chest. Whitewashed, very low curbstones.

Natasha, the interpreter, slender from the waist up, broad-beamed from the waist down, with hazel eyes set far apart, eyes that reminded Sid of Jackie Kennedy Onassis, asked three town residents the whereabouts of Ko*tov*skogo Street, where Sid's first cousin, Riva, lived. They said they didn't know. "Ask them where the post office is," Sid suggested. Again the residents professed ignorance. The van moved along slowly. On the right he saw a small park surrounded by a black iron fence.

"That's my park!" he cried. "Stop!"

Peter parked the van nearby, and he and Natasha waited in it while the Littles and Helen had a look at the place, Sid feeling claustrophobic because of Helen's insistent presence. Neatly dressed, smiling school kids slowly walking in single file. A white statue of Lenin glowering in a suit and long overcoat, as if he was cold on this twenty-third of May. Vividly painted concrete gnomes here and there. A kiosk with a red metal roof, and a young woman selling ice cream. Acacia blossoms in clusters on the walks. Maples, elms. Standing as if transfixed, Sid stared at the gazebo, the bandstand and the small restaurant, all of which he had last seen some sixty years ago.

Ice cream outdoors, summer night, band music. How glorious they were! Little Sidney and his mom and dad were sitting at a wooden table, eating rose ice cream, his favorite. The waiter in his white jacket bowed before him. Sidney's dad slipped Sidney a coin, and Sidney tipped the man. A little blond girl in blue, sitting with her mom and dad at a nearby table. Sidney's mom, looking dreamy, nodding to the music's beat. The air sweet with acacia blossoms. Sidney's dad, sitting like a general, fingering his waxed handlebar mustache.

A summer house. Sea smells. Irises. His mom was reading to him about boys at a boarding school, and about a teacher standing behind a high desk. Poppy meadows covered by plants waving cups on their long stems. He knew how to break open cups and eat the dry seeds while staring at the waving plants and rolling meadows.

His mom had warned him not to eat too many. The meadows came up short against cool woods. Her voice grew distant, faint, a delicious murmur.

In Sidney's courtyard were thick vines. At times the grapes were green, at others purple. What a wonderful life they led. When Sidney was hot and the jams in the cauldrons were bubbling, the vines with their large, rough leaves looked cool.

"Dad, are these our vines?" he asked.

"Yes."

"I like them. Sometimes even better than ice cream."

"Better than rose ice cream?"

"No."

"Our vines," thought Sidney. What would his courtyard be without them?

Sidney's tall, skinny, unmarried Aunt Celia, his dad's oldest sister, with the frizzy, thick dark hair, often kissed him wetly and insistently, causing him to squirm and wipe his cheek.

"Be nice to her," said his mom. "She adores you."

But later, at home, he overheard her say to his dad, "I wish you'd ask her not to kiss him like that. Doesn't she see it upsets him?"

"He's a devil," said his dad. "He persecutes her, knowing how much she loves him."

The other day a peasant kissed his old mom on the street near Sidney's courtyard. He must have been drunk, because when she disappeared around the corner he spat at the cobblestones.

"Next time she kisses me wetly I'll spit just like that," thought Sidney.

In the park now, Sid Little had become aware of a strong odor of urine, the kind he had recently experienced in Moscow, Kharkov, Kiev. Curious, he followed the smell to an underground toilet suggesting a wartime bunker, descended a long flight of concrete steps, made a sharp left turn and was embraced by darkness hovering above a gleaming, wet concrete floor. Mottled tile walls. On the right, a long ceramic container like a cattle feeding trough, aflood with a green-golden liquid. Sickly blue stalls showing dark, gleaming stains. No sign of toilet paper. Thinking of the political and economic connections between this toilet's present state and the condition of Kharkov's and Kiev's Stalinesque buildings, he returned to Doris and Helen, and they all rejoined the van.

Though driving aimlessly, Peter stumbled upon Sid's cousin's house, let his four passengers out, and drove off somewhere. Sid, closely followed by Helen, was the first to step over a sliding-gate rail and enter the courtyard, in which several men and women were chatting. A barking, bounding, snarling collie mutt on an old rope was beside herself because he was out of reach of her fangs. He was aware of old red bricks, faded fence palings, ancient potted plants, a battered piano stool, rotting irregular planks, and little plastic bags drying on a laundry line.

Natasha, after a brief exchange in Russian, introduced him and Doris to an embarrassed, attractive, buxom woman in a dress with a leaf-and-flower motif, who knew no English and little Yiddish and whom he took, correctly, to be his Cousin Riva. Helen introduced herself. Riva was probably sixty. Hair dyed black. An incisor encased in gold. After embracing her, the Littles and Helen met her second husband, Joseph, and Joseph's grandson, Boris, the latter about fourteen. Joseph, in a gray suit whose lapel sported a round military medal, and wearing a peach shirt and diagonally striped tie, said something in Russian to Boris, and Boris locked the dog in a small shed, whereupon the mutt poked her black nose in the space under the shed door, repeatedly snapped her jaws, bit only air, and howled in frustration.

Following Riva and Joseph, the visitors brushed aside a curtain and entered a living room. There followed an explosion of feverish hospitality, for it seemed that nothing short of a miracle had occurred. Riva and Joseph, expecting the Littles *tomorrow*, had prepared a feast in advance. Not only that. They were expecting a visit this very afternoon from Riva's younger sister and her husband from San Jose in America, where they had been living the past eight years. Consequently what expressions of Russian-Jewish love for the prematurely arrived American relatives! What a babel and frustration of tongues, Riva, Joseph and Helen speaking Russian and only a trifling amount of Yiddish; Sid speaking English and passable Yiddish; Natasha speaking Russian and broken English; and Doris struck dumb! Joseph turned off the large TV. A white linen tablecloth was spread on the large rectangular table, and dishes and utensils were heaped noisily on it. Platters of food and drink emerged rapidly from another room, carried lovingly with oil-wet hands by Riva. Soviet vodka, Soviet beer, Ceylon tea, Dnieper herring, baby lamb, black bread, Soviet chocolate.

And now, adding to the tumult, the two San Jose relatives, Anna and Sergei, arrived, whom Sid had never met. Cousin Anna promptly kissed Sid on the mouth. Anna's rosy, prominent cheeks gave the impression she was jolly, although her eyes, showing too much white, were a little too large, as if goiter was lurking behind them. She was of middle height, whereas Sergei, saturnine, owlish, was tall, thick, a Russian bear. Sergei crushed Sid's hand with his meaty paw in a show of familial warmth. Thereupon dapper Little Sid Little, sixty-three, of Roslyn, Long Island, the Little Sid Little who had recently had a second and glorious bar mitzvah, the Sid Little who was a former attorney in negligence law, and a former compensation-case judge in the State of New York (compensation-case referee, rather), announced that he must leave at once to do what he had come so far to do—to wander the streets of Akkerman/Belgorod—and he said it quickly, in staccato, in his deep, resonant, firm voice.

"My bar mitzvah boy!" cried Doris ironically and aggressively. This was the same Doris who, with her short, mannish-looking, brass-golden hair and athletic, youthful figure, could at times look vulnerable, pathetic. And tall, solidly built Helen of the purple irises, Helen the chemist or pediatrician or gynecologist or whatever, Helen of the wild, dyed, henna hair, Odessa Helen who was a sister-in-law of Sid's second cousin, said something sternly and loudly in Russian while staring at him.

In addition to Doris's and Helen's reactions, his announcement was greeted by Russian astonishment, puzzlement and confusion. Cousin Riva offered him vodka, baby lamb, Russian beer, homemade cake, a glass of hot tea. And then—it was unbelievable, it was almost more than he could politely endure—Riva thrust a wet tidbit of baby lamb into his mouth and, almost choking in surprise, he had to chew and swallow it. And Doris, who had been so skeptical about Nora Gallagher's actually shoving wet food and wet long fingers into his mouth, and doing it not once, not twice, but thrice, was now witnessing that such a thing could indeed happen to him—again! (He remembered Nora's short blond hair, her bold, almost mannish smiles, her uneven, brilliant, strong teeth.)

But Sid Little, of middle height, looking affluent, dignified, quietly authoritative, looking well preserved, and even jolly despite his aquiline features and his various anxieties (nowadays he was no longer on easy terms with his body and his God), wasn't going to be put off by such reactions. For he was very eager to explore neighboring streets in his quest for lost childhood memories, and was uncomfortably aware that the Belgorod-Dniestrovski outing was all too brief, Intourist having allotted two or three hours to the town at most. After all, he told himself as he made his way out of the house, how would he account to his conscience, later when he was back in Roslyn, Long Island, if he chose to socialize instead of trying to see as much of old Akkerman as he could?

"KOTOVSKOGO/26-22," said the plaque attached to a wall of a corner building. However, it was in Cyrillic, which he couldn't read, so he was aware that he mustn't get lost, for he was unable to say what Riva's surname was. Impatient, and hopeful that a house or courtyard might bring back more lost memories, he turned to the right and strode rapidly down the empty, unlittered gutter until the street ended at right angles to another. A glary day, shadows vaguely defined. Very low curbstones. Asphalt sidewalks, cracked, pitted, chunks missing. Windblown ivory acacia clusters nestling against curbs.

Carefully noting landmarks, he retraced his way and tried other deserted streets. Curbs empty of vehicles. Overarching elms and acacias. Perspectives of green trees and whitewashed ashen tree trunks. Street hand-pumps with long iron handles. Elderly women pumping water into buckets. Most of the houses were earth-color stucco and in mediocre condition, but several, of brick or stone, looked in good shape. A few of the houses, abandoned, showed smashed windows and sky-leaking roof holes. Wheel-like roof antennas on tall metal poles, the wheels suggesting UFOs. A small boy inside a hoop, whirling it around his hips, studying him. A stout woman, carrying a large metal tub, stepped onto the receiving platform of what Sid took to be a nursing home and hurled dirty water onto a barren yard.

If there was anything in this world little Sidney hated it was penka, the loathsome skin that floated on overheated milk and fouled his mouth. He would spit it out wildly.

"Penka! Penka!" he would shout.

"Now look here!" said his mom grimly one day, face reddening. "The time has come to make you eat it! Eat it!"

He threw himself on the floor, grew rigid, wailed like a banshee.

"All right!" she cried. "I won't ask you to eat it again."

Now he was sad, because she was staring, and looking pained and perplexed.

"Mom, please don't be sad."

Shrivelled peppers hanging by a sunlit door.

"I want to touch them," he said.

"Better not," she said.

"I need to."

"Do. Do," she said.

He touched them, forgot, rubbed his eyes, and howled as his eyes burned.

"Do. Do," she said.

She was pacing the bedroom floor. Suddenly she ran to the bed, fetched the chamber pot from under it, lifted up her skirt, pulled down her drawers, squatted, exploded. A brown cannonball flew across the room and hit a wall. Another spattered on the polished floor. What fun! Only a grownup was strong enough to do that.

His dad's dad, whom Sidney called Pampie, had a poor little store. Kegs (not barrels) of herring. Kegs (not barrels) of pickles. Dried fish. Wood. Kerosene. Barley. At times Pampie's eyes, observing him, gleamed out of his dark face with its dark beard.

"Dead fish don't bite!" Pampie would shout. "Touch them! Touch everything! Run around the counter! Faster!"

Little Sidney liked to do as he was told, but afterwards, at home, he was puzzled. Why was he full of thoughts, and so few answers?

It was a hot, dusty day. Soldiers were chatting in Sidney's courtyard. A young soldier came in off the street, face angry, wet. He was crying! He said something bitterly to his comrades. Then, with a furious gesture, he turned one of his trouser pockets inside out. He had been robbed! Little Sidney cried too, because the pocket contained some tobacco flakes, one of which flew into his eye, burning it. He ran into the house as the soldiers laughed.

In summer the sea was all-important to little Sidney. There was the Black Sea, stormy, dark. And the little sea, an inlet separated from the great sea by a long sand strip. Using his large hands, his dad would scoop up blobs of fat, black, stinking mud and smear them on Sidney. Sidney would squirm, make anguished faces.

"Be still! It's good for you," said his dad.

"You like it?"

"Of course."

"It stinks."

"A healthy stink," said his dad, spreading some mud on his hairy chest.

The smell flew up Sidney's nostrils, making him wheeze. Lying still, he could hear the baking mud squeak. Translucent, tea-colored pearls of sweat rose from cracks in the mud drying on him. His dad led him into the sea, splashed cold water over him, and Sidney felt he was his dad's true heir, because he shared his dad's mud, sand, sea. He believed his dad was grooming him for a great role in the wide world some day.

Sidney spotted a tiny swimming fish, caught it, brought it triumphantly to his dad.

"Nice," said his dad vaguely, gazing at a woman on the beach.

Sidney studied the fish. "Yes," he thought, "I'm a great catcher of fish. Life is very pleasant this morning."

Sidney and his mom and dad were on the Black Sea beach. A storm blew up. They hurried to the carriage. Making too sharp a turn, the carriage fell on its side. They crawled out. Sidney's dad shouted at the peasant driver. The carriage was righted. The driver shouted at the neighing horses. A frightening, magical experience.

Sidney and Dad were taking a long walk. Very long. Climbing, climbing a hill. Far below were farms, white steeples, a village.

"You love this hill, Dad?" he asked.

"Yes."

"Me too."

He gave Dad his hand as a reward.

He and his dad were near the strong-smelling Black Sea. It was a hot, very still day. The countryside spread out around them. The boat man, who had rowed them across the lake, had failed to show up. So they walked, walked, walked.

"Be brave, my boy," said his dad.

The water sparkled brutally. Village steeples. Geese. Old men with creased eyes and wet mustaches. And his dad high above him, legs working like pistons.

"Brute. Fool. How dare you make us walk?" his dad muttered.

"Maybe he's sick?"

Hot, tired, but smiling, his dad said, "He's given us a good hike, anyway. We'll have some ice cream when we get home."

The rest of the walk was bitter with sweat.

Sid Little's parents had walked these streets, had perhaps visited some of these houses. This was supposedly *his* town, for he had lived important years here. But on this visit here with Doris it was not his town any longer. It was a different town now. Where were the banks of purple irises with their heady perfume that had hypnotized him as a child, made him spacey? And the hot, gently rolling poppy fields? And the carriage rides and the slow clop of hooves? And the stable smells, and the crack of whips? And the cellar smells of barrelled pickles, pickled tomatoes, sauerkraut, acrid potatoes, acrid dirt floor? And the estuary smells, the rich mud smells, the raw green sea smells? He thought he knew where many of those smells had gone. Smog was pervasive in Moscow, Kiev, Odessa; on the highway between Odessa and here; and even in the environs of this old town. And his elderly nostrils had been assailed by the fumes of the pale green Intourist van.

His fear of encountering a soldier, or a cop, or some bureaucratic local aparatchik, and of being asked to account for himself, had been unwarranted, as it had turned out. Although people had seen him (at one intersection he had exchanged glances with a couple of young soldiers), no one had hindered him. There was a Gorbachev change in the Soviet air, palpable even in this quiet, old, Bessarabian town so meaningful in his personal history. But what was the meaning of the return of his childhood memories? And of what use were they to him now that he had them back? Did he feel like a fuller person? No. A richer? No. A wiser? No. So what was the point of having quested for them? He didn't know. "Be humble. Your destiny is the worm," he told himself, remembering Dick Gallagher.

He went to a nearby, newer, larger park, where young soldiers and girls were strolling separately. A stout, middle-aged woman wearing a babushka asked him, "Are you American?" Her teeth shone with stainless steel. Her face was very lean. The strange light in her eyes disturbed him. "I show you history Belgorod. I make you happy. Very cheap." "No thank you," he said, stepping into the gutter, and proceeded to Riva's, where the mutt, on her rope again, was beside herself trying to defend the yard against him. Young Boris ran out of the house and threatened the dog with a huge chunk of wood. The snarling changed to a muted gargling as the whites of the collie's eyes bulged with frustration.

"So how was it you were helped by the Russians to escape to the Urals?" Doris was asking Anna as Sid joined her on the sofa. "Weren't the Russians anti-Semitic?"

"It was not anti-Semitism in the Soviet Union," said Sergei loudly, glancing at Sid. "I guarantee you was not anti-Semitism. Stalin was supporter of the Jews. I guarantee you a hundred percent."

"What about the doctors' plot? Didn't he want to have a lot of Jewish doctors killed?" Doris asked Anna.

Smiling happily, Cousin Riva handed Sid a bowl of cold borscht containing a dollop of sour cream, then motioned to a large, heavy plate on the table, on which were spread baby lamb, potatoes, cooked cabbage and black bread. Beginning to eat, he realized his Akkerman wanderings had worked up an appetite.

"I'm talking from 1917 to 1941," said Sergei forcefully. "When the war began, after Stalin became friend of Hitler, and when Hitler began war against Stalin, against Communists and Jews and Gypsies—he killed them right away. In the beginning of war, in Soviet Union it was no anti-Semitic. It was huge patriotism in country. So Soviet government said to everybody, 'Leave, because the Germans they gonna kill you, and this and that and that.' *But* (it was a but) in the beginning of war were rumors that Germans they kill Jews. And a lot of people couldn't believe."

"Doris asking *me*. Why you talk?" Anna asked Sergei, smiling.

"Doris, I'm telling you story about my father," said Sergei, opening his eyes wide and again glancing at Sid. "He was in service from 1910. In Czar army. He was serving in Warsaw. 1914 begins the war. He was wounded, so he became war prisoner. And he used to live in Germany. And he used to work with farmers. And he was okay. Everything was okay. Even translators from Russian to German was a lot of Jews because very similar language. And they was treating Jews very well. Everything was fine. And my father couldn't believe. He said, 'Germans can't kill Jews. I'm a witness. I know about that. I used to live there.' In 1941 he was already fifty-five years old. And he wouldn't go to war, to service, nothing. So, my first cousin, his nephew, he was bigshot in Odessa during beginning of war, and he realized that, if we going to stay in Odessa when Germans were arrived in Odessa, they gonna kill us immediately. So he took everybody in his car. And we couldn't take luggage with us. It was at that time it was a small car, with an open top. And he came to the ship. And it was a line. The people stood from ship about half a city. So, he came to the captain, and he said, 'Here's my ID, and so and so.' And the captain said, '*That* people should go on the ship.' "

"In Akkerman was another story," said Anna. "In Akkerman from 1918 till 1940 was Romanian government. In 1940 came—"

"In 1940 came Communists," interrupted Sergei. "Not everybody was happy with Russian people when they came to Bessarabia. And, when supposed to come Hitler, they say, 'We are friends to Romania. The Germans they will come in Akkerman and everything will be fine. We don't want to go away. We will stay here. We have friends from Romania. And they will not kill us.' "

"He interrupts me," said Anna, smiling. "Now be quiet, Sergei, and let me say. My grandfather and my grandmother say, 'Romanians come. We are old people. They will never touch us. Everything will be the same what was before 1940. We will not go.' But my mother was very smart woman. And she say, 'I don't trust Romanians. I know Hitler will kill us and my children. We supposed to go— anywhere, but not here.' And she took me, my sister, my father. And we left to U*ral*. And during 1941 to 1945 we stay in U*ral*. When

Hitler came in Akkerman, they put all Jewish people (and my grand-father and grandmother) in synagogue in Akkerman. They put kerosene. And they fire all Jewish people. Old. Young. Everybody. In that synagogue. My Aunts Yetta and Sophie were in Odessa. And people saw them. Then they saw them in concentration camp. And after the war we didn't find them. So I think Hitler killed them."

Little Sidney marching, marching on an iron-grilled balcony, with a stick on his shoulder and with his Astrakhan hat shining glo-riously and smelling of sheep. And morning in Siberia. And Sidney and his mom in his dad's barracks room. His dad away somewhere.

"I'm hungry! Hungry!" cried Sidney, emptiness gnawing at his gut.

"Sh!" his mom whispered.

"I'm hungry! Hungry!" the officer next door, stepping into the corridor, mimicked nasally, face white with lather. He wore trousers but no shirt.

One day Sidney placed two silver rings on the wood stove. When he went to fetch them they were blobs, not rings.

"Mama, something terrible happened to my rings!" he cried.

"Children's rings melt if they're heated," said his mom. "When you get a grownup's ring it won't matter if you leave it on the stove."

"I don't like children's rings," he said.

His Uncle Alex, a watchmaker, was a funny man with a jolly face, large brown eyes and a large brown mustache. Grownups laughed whenever they spoke about Uncle Alex. Sometimes Uncle Alex became an actor in a crowded little theater. People flitted across the stage, gesturing violently. Then a figure waving a little flag leaped through a door at the back and everybody laughed be-cause it was Uncle Alex, eyes sparkling, mustache shining. What was the little flag for? And why was he, a watchmaker, doing this?

"How long did it take to go to the Urals?" asked Sid, fingering the ancient scar above his right eyebrow.

"Long time, long time," said Sergei, shifting his heavy weight on his wooden chair.

"Maybe two weeks," said Cousin Anna.

"Why so long?" asked Sid.

"We go in small freight cars for horses," Anna said. "They put two shelves. And twenty-five, thirty families stay on these shelves. I was eight years old. My sister, Riva, eleven. My mother was forty-one. Father forty-one. On the train they put little heaters and chimneys. And each station come Russian people and bring us a little soup, a little kasha. And we eat what people give us, because nobody has money. Nothing. And each station Russian people from villages and cities they come and help us." Anna paused. "We lost my sister, Riva," she continued, glancing at Riva, who was speaking in Russian with Helen.

"Lost her?" asked Sid, also glancing at Riva.

"We supposed to take a little water to make tea," said Anna. "And after five minutes, train move-it. And it's no my sister. No Riva. So . . . train move-it two days. And no Riva. After few days there is another train. And she took-it that train. And it was open platform. And she came. She was all black. Face and hands and everything. She found-it us. I don't know *how* she found-it us. It was miracle!"

"What was the toilet situation on the train?" asked Sid.

"I will tell you toilet situation," said Sergei loudly, leaning forward and frowning. "The toilet situation was, when the train stopped, he could stay, for example, three or four hours. He could move five miles and stop for one hour. He could move a hundred miles and stop for five minutes. So people walked out from cars. And wherever they could find out a place, *there* was toilet situation."

"One man, very old, is blind," said Anna. "And he pee between carriages. His wife screaming, 'Why you pee there? You be killed! Pee in car!'"

The market! Carts! Horses! Donkeys! Goats! Peasants shouting, flies biting! Sidney was standing outside a store. A blind man bumped into him, almost falling.

"Blind pig! Watch where you're going!" shouted a man Sidney didn't know.

Was the man joking? The blind man, poorly dressed, muttered an apology. Sidney glanced at his face. Was blindness evil?

Sidney was sitting with his mom on a courtyard bench. Smells of dirt, barn, chickens. A hen leaped onto his lap, scaring him.

"Don't be afraid," said his mom. "She wants to be your friend. Pat her. That's right."

"Do the others want to be my friend?"

"No."

"Why?"

"She's different. She was in the barn with a lot of the others. A skunk came in one night and stifled them all except her. So now she needs to sit on your lap. Let her do it. Don't let a creature be lonely."

The hen nestled on his lap like a cat.

"Chicken, chicken," he murmured, patting her. "What's a skunk?" he asked.

"An animal that gives off a very bad smell."

"Is it large?"

"No."

"Will it stifle me?"

"No."

"Why did it stifle the chickens?"

"Maybe the roosters attacked it."

"Chicken, chicken," he murmured.

Afterwards, when he called to the hen she jumped on his lap to be patted.

Whenever Sidney visited Gram he immediately asked her to prepare the reins, a rope tied to a bedpost. Then he was off, flying over roads, meadows, through deep woods.

"Whoa!" he shouted, tugging, or "Giddyap!" as he cracked an imaginary whip.

When his mom and dad were ready to leave, they persuaded him to stop driving. Then, like a peasant stiff from a long wagon trip, he walked home between them with that slight waddle one got from driving certain wagons.

"Didn't they have pails and buckets?" asked Sid.

"Was no place. No space for this," said Sergei.

"It was maybe twelve family in one carriage," said Anna.

"Was there any sex on this train?" asked Sid.

"Let me make clear the situation," said Sergei, turning to Sid. "It was a tragedy. The nation was in a tragedy. *After* was sex, but during—"

"With me there would have been sex," said Sid, deadpan.

"We talking about Nathanson family," Cousin Anna said, grinning. "Forget about *your* family. I will tell you about Mike, my father's brother, ten years older. This man was number one in our family who loved sex. If wife or not wife doesn't matter."

"Forgive me, Sid and Doris, for my word, but he was a sex bandit," said Sergei.

"After war," said Cousin Anna (Sid noticed her faint mustache), "Mike and my father, when they came in Akkerman, they live together. And one-half part of house was my father and mother. Another half was Mike with a woman. His wife. But that was third wife. Official wife. But it was hundred other wives *un*official. So if you ask-it about sex, Mike was the kid. He used to love Goy women."

"He was very smart man! He could do anything!" said Sergei, eyes bulging. "And very good-looking. The women they loved him. And he knew how to make money. He was very strong. Could lift big—"

"He had a tragedy," interrupted Anna.

"A tragedy?" Sid asked.

"Big tragedy!" said Sergei loudly. "I will tell you about it."

"He interrupts me," Anna said. "Please, Sergei. He had a wife after war. Third wife. The last wife. A Goy. And she had a daughter. That daughter married. She—"

"Anna, she had twins, boy and girl," said Sergei.

"No, no," said Anna. "With first husband she had two boys. With second she had two girls, twins. And one time came that first husband from Moscow. He was living in Moscow. And he said, 'Leave your second husband and come back to me.' So she went with him to Moscow. One day she came back to Akkerman with that first husband to take money from the bank—mother money, Mike money. And she took all the money. And somebody from the bank called second husband, because all children was with second husband."

"All children?" asked Doris. "Even from the first husband?"

"Yes!" Sergei said loudly. "Second husband was a very nice man!"

"Second husband took a rifle. And he killed her. And he killed himself," said Anna quietly.

"Wow," Doris said.

The lady who taught little Sidney French said, "La lampe, le crayon." But he was afraid of being deserted by Grampa, his mom's dad, who accompanied him across fields to the lady's house. He didn't trust Grampa, with his long tea-colored mustache and long beard. He begged Grampa to walk ahead of him so he could keep an eye on him. But Grampa stubbornly lagged behind, studying the ground. They walked close to water, and beached boats, and smells of nets, and rough male voices. Thoughts of the little girl in blue.

Sometimes Sidney's mom and dad went to a ball, leaving Sidney alone with Grampa. Parents went to balls, that was the rule. But Sidney couldn't figure out this thing about balls. He had studied telephone poles, but had never seen musicians and dancers up there on them. So what kind of game was that? The poles were high. If a dancing grownup fell off, he or she might be killed.

"Grampa. The balls are on the telephone poles?"

Grampa stared at him from under bushy gray eyebrows. "True."

"Have you been on the poles?"

"Long ago."

What could it mean? It was certainly true there were balls on the poles—the grownups said so. But it was just as true that Sidney couldn't understand it, no matter how hard he tried.

"Let's get back to the Urals," said Doris Little after a pause.

"So, we all together on this train," said Cousin Anna. "And first we came to Magnitogorsk. We stay there, because they make a bridge there. And my father working, a cashier. He pay salary to people who working to construct bridges and railroads. They finish a bridge, they move. We live not far from this where they make bridges. There was very nice Russian people. We came very dirty. We came after two weeks we travel in that car. We didn't wash for two weeks. We have lousy. We have no spoon. And people make a bath for us. They have no hot water in house. It was a small house in *back* yard. And they made there hot water and put us all together. And they wash-it us. They gave us a pillow. A blanket. Everything. They move in kitchen and they give us living room. We pay a little money. But on that time there was very little money. And then my mother start to work. One thing she could take-it from home it was my father's, a case for cigarettes. Very expensive. Expensive stones. And gold and silver. And she gave this to one woman. And the woman gave her a sewing machine. And my mother start to make clothes for this people. And they gave us food. For example, for a dress they gave a barrel of potato. Another bring a chicken. Another a dozen of eggs, a little flour. And she start to work. And we have everything."

"So if the Soviet Union hadn't retaken Bessarabia from Romania in 1940, you and your sister would probably have been killed by the Germans?" said Sid to Cousin Anna.

"Correct," replied Sergei.

"Did you go to the Urals too?" Sid asked Sergei.

"No. Tashkent."

"Tashkent? That must have been a long journey."

"Six, seven days by train."

"How long did you stay in Magnitogorsk?" Doris asked Anna.

"In Magnitogorsk we stay about two years," said Anna.

"And then?"

"Then we left Magnitogorsk about 1943. And we move to another place. To Sovsva, not far from Sverdlovsk. It was a small village, Sovsva. This was end of railroad. No more railroad. No more bridges. Tai*ga*—forest."

"Frontier," said Sergei, smiling.

"First went my father," said Anna. "And then we come after a few months. There was no houses. They make bridges but there was no houses. And they make underground a small room. And cover this room. Make a heater there. And we stay all together in this place. With our family was my mother's sister. She was very good cook. And she start to work in diner, where workmen eat. And from diner she brought a little food for us. And from first day my mother say, 'War is war, but children supposed to go in school.' And so from first day me and Riva we was in school. One spring time it was water come on this road, and we couldn't come back, so we stay in that village where was school. We stay ten days. We stay in school, me and Riva. And Russian people come and bring us food."

"What was your father doing?" asked Doris.

"My father he was on that time manager in warehouse, where was kerosene and everything what they need to make this bridges. Nails. Kerosene. Wood. This stuff. Not far from this place where he work and we live, was village. My mother went to this village and start to make dresses and coat. And people gave potato, butter. And my mother say, 'You supposed to go in school.' But school was very far. It was thirteen kilometers."

"Eight miles," said Sergei.

"And we walk with my sister two hours," said Anna. "And my mother take a room for us. And we stay all week there. In winter was okay. It was snow, and we walking. But in spring time you supposed to stop every kilometer and clean your boot. Because you can't walk, you have so big mud. These thirteen kilometers nobody. No villages. No people. I was eleven. Riva already fourteen. My mother stay in village all week. And my father was working on this place where they make bridges and everything."

"Did you have a boyfriend?" asked Sid.

"Yes. We study together. We go to school together. We play together. And we go on the forest to ski. We were like children in America. Same thing."

"Was he Jewish?" asked Doris.

"No. There no Jews."

"Did you visit your classmates in their homes?" asked Doris.

"Very often. They have no fathers. Everybody was on the front. They have only women and children and old people. And people who make bridges and railroads. Who have special permission to stay in Ural. And that time, of course, women with husband in army they have friends. And friends come to have sex with this women. Regular. *People are people*. Many men have no wives. We was with our father. Where was our father, was our mother. He was only few months without us. And when we came, he was like this." She held up a forefinger. "He have no food. He no practical. For example, people can give a bottle of kerosene and take a barrel of potato. My father very honest. I say, 'Papa, give me please a little kerosene. I can't do my classes. Is dark in our house.' He say, 'I can't give you. I give you a little only to make classes, no more. This not belong to me. I will not give you.'"

"Did Riva have a boyfriend?" asked Sid, glancing at Riva, who was speaking with Joseph, her husband.

"She was very beautiful. And she have a lot boyfriends. She was like Mike."

Laughter.

"Did you have entertainment? Dances?" asked Sid.

"In same diner where during day come people from work and have dinner, there in night time they have accordion, they have everything. Of course, no piano. And they dance-it. My sister was older. *She* dance-it. I just look-it. In same diner they show movies at night time. First they show movie about war. Many movie was at that time about war. And after movie was dancing."

"Did you have a sense of what was happening in the concentration camps?" asked Sid.

"Only rumors," said Sergei.

"It was no radio in home," said Anna. "It was radio in the street. We get news from the street."

"Did you stay in the Urals until the end of the war?" asked Doris.

"No," said Cousin Anna. "In 1944 we moved to Dnepropetrovsk. During war there was Hitler. But in 1944 Hitler move-it from Ukraine. We went to make a new bridge on the Dnieper. And there was city, Dnepropetrovsk. Not far from Dnepropetrovsk was a village, Eegren. And there we stay until war finish. In 1945, when war finish, we in Eegren. In Akkerman came Abram Karolik, our friend. And he send a letter to my mother that our building in Akkerman is broken, so we have no house in Akkerman. And my mother made decision to go after war to Odessa. We stop-it in Odessa. And my father was working in Odessa. And then he had three heart attacks. We used to live on third floor, and there was no elevator. And doctor came and said to my mother, 'If you want have your husband alive, move from third floor.' And then Mike said, 'Let we make a house together in Akkerman.' Mike have a little money on that time. My mother have a little. And father a little. And they build new house in Akkerman one block from railway station."

"So after the war *you* didn't go back to Akkerman," Sid said.

"No. Because our house is destroyed."

"So when did Riva go back to Akkerman?" asked Sid.

"Riva's husband was working in Lithuania. And she stay with him in Lithuania. And he was KGB man. And one day they say, 'You supposed to make a choice. Your wife or your job.' Because she had relatives in the United States. So he was dismissed. He left Lithuania, beautiful apartment, and came to Odessa. We had little apartment. And father was sick. He was long time in bed. And my sister said, 'Odessa is not for us. We can't stay here. We supposed to go in Akkerman, where is Mike. Mike will help us.' And Riva found apartment. And Riva live in apartment."

"When the Jews came back to Akkerman after the war, was there anti-Semitism?" asked Doris.

"Why not?" said Sergei.

"Not everybody anti-Semitic," Anna said. "My mother had friends in Akkerman. They had a big farm of grapes before war. And one winter was very cold. Everything frozen. They came to my mother and said, 'Give me money.' All Christmas, all New Year, we celebrate with these Russian people. And my mother gave a lot of money. They start to produce again grapes, again wine, and were very rich people. When we left in 1940 they say, 'Don't worry. You will come back. Your house will be all right.' And during war they put cross on our house, that we are Russian, not Jewish. So nobody touch-it our house. And 1945, before we came, Russians already came, soldiers. Somebody destroyed the house. When Abram write we have no more house, it was terrible for my mother, because it was brand-new house. And these Russian friends they say, 'What can we do? To the last days it was okay your house. We take care all four years of your house.' And then they gave us pillows. Blankets. Everything. Because we have nothing. We came after war we have nothing. And they help us. And they friendly all years. All years they friendly. Of course, it was people who, for example, you are Jewish, it was war, and a neighbor come and say, 'You know, he's Jewish.' How Hitler can know you are Jewish? *Neighbor say!* But many neighbors put in their basement Jewish people, and they stay there four years. One person, when he went from this basement after four years, he can't look on the street. He can't walk, is blind. It was people like this also."

"When the Jews came back to Akkerman there was no synagogue?" Sid asked.

"No," said Sergei.

"They meet in apartment, and friends go each to another," said Anna.

"Did the Germans do a lot of damage to Akkerman?" asked Sid.

"Yes," said Anna.

"Did they damage the Jewish cemetery?"

"Everything was broken."

"Did the Jews get their property back?"

"The land belongs to government. Our house is destroyed. So they don't give us any place. That's *it!*"

"What are the most unpleasant memories of your life in the Urals?" Doris asked Anna.

"When I walk with my mother to village where she was working, and I study in that village," Anna replied. "It was very cold. Nobody was on street. And when we came on this village, people ask us, 'How you still alive? Is so cold! How you walk?' And my mother said, 'Because I have to work. Because my family needs food. And *she's* supposed to go in school, because she's supposed to study.' My mother never finished school. She always push us to study. '*I* didn't finish college, but *you* supposed to finish college.'"

"What are your most *pleasant* memories?" asked Sid.

Anna thought a while.

"When came with my sister from school home for whole week," she said. "In village where school is, Riva prepare every day the same soup. She prepare soup from potato and cream farina. She put a few potatoes. She put cream farina and fried onion. And if we have carrots. . . . Not always we have carrots. And we have a piece of bread. But my mother give us much more. And when we come, my mother is waiting. . . ."

Cousin Anna 's lips trembled. Her head drooped. She looked anguished. She began to cry silently.

"It was hard," she said, looking up and fingering away tears. "Thirteen kilometers alone with Riva through forest. . . . It was already dark.

. . . My mother so glad to see us. . . . She said, 'How nice children! You are here already! I *see* you!' It was so clean. And underground. From gauze she made curtains on the windows. It was clean. It was warm. It was delicious varenikas with potatoes."

She started to cry again.

"It was *best* time in U*ral*," she said after a while.

"So much misery, past and present," thought Sid, remembering Dick Gallagher.

It was time for the Odessa group to leave. It was a gorgeous day, so at Sid's suggestion the group, before returning to the city, visited Belgorod's citadel, which overlooked the lake-like, sparkling Dniester estuary just outside of town. Peter, the driver, stayed in the van. Natasha, still wearing pink ballet-type slippers though the group had some walking to do, said this was one of the largest fortresses in the Ukraine region, with four gates, twenty-six towers, and walls more than a mile and a quarter long. It had been built from the thirteenth to the fifteenth centuries and had been repaired and its outer moat deepened in the sixteenth and seventeenth. The huge stone walls, in places weathered by what looked like seaspray, were a somber, ashen gray. Time and the maritime climate had caused the top of some of them to crumble.

Crossing a landbridge that had replaced the drawbridge, the group entered the extensive, flat, lowland area enclosed by the wandering walls. Giddying, rail-less stone stairways. Squat cylindrical towers. A huge naked chimney. Clumps of trees with whitewashed trunks. Dniester views. Shiny cobbled wagon trails disappearing in undergrowth in a flowering meadow. Pink flowers. Pink-flowering bushes. Estuary smells. Signs of wooden stairways that had once clung to stone walls. Dungeons. Keeps. Pits. A blue sky. A ringing silence.

At one point, when Sid and Doris were alone together, Sid asked, "Anything interesting happen during my absence?"

Doris laughed.

"Natasha delicately starts picking away at the baby lamb," she said. "So does Helen. Between them they *kill* it. I timidly said to Natasha, 'I'd like you to ask Riva a question for me.' She said, '*Just a moment*! I'm speaking to Helen!' like she's a member of the family. Riva brings out this box of chocolates and opens it. The chocolate has a grayish color. I didn't have my glasses on, but I started to see little things crawling out of it—ants. They probably had been cooped up for years. I didn't want Riva and Joseph to be embarrassed, so I tried to corral about eight of them with the under side of a plate. Riva probably thought I was having Saint Vitus' dance. She lifts the plate up to see what's under it, and they scoot all over the table. It was very embarrassing. Riva brings out a huge cake, with whipped cream. Helen gets hold of a wedge about *this big*, then reaches for another. Riva gives me a gift package, and I hold it vertically, and six soup spoons hit the floor. I didn't know there was anything wrapped up in it, it looked like a tablecloth. In addition to the spoons, there's enough material to make a dress. Which shows they have so little conception of what we have in our country. It was very touching."

Lately, little Sidney's dad went every few days to a distant street, saw a man at a certain hour, and came home looking upset.

"Dad, where did you go?" asked Sidney.

"To see an official. To get permission for us to go to America."

"What's an official?"

"A man who can give us permission."

His dad said to his mom, "The swine kept me waiting two hours. Once they know you want to leave, they don't care how they treat you, especially if you're a Jew. Two hours to tell me no word has come yet. 'Your honor, you know I'll make it worth your while if you speed things up,' I say. He winks and laughs. 'Who's worried?' he says, and I leave without spitting in his eye. Romania!"

Little Sidney's important dad went to an unknown street to be mistreated. Why did the official insult him?

Riding on trains, rolling, bumping, creaking. Shawls, mustaches, beards. Sidney's dad, busy with tickets, schedules, conductors, papers, was often silent. Riding, riding. From darkness into light, light into darkness.

"We're crossing Europe," said Sidney's mom.

"A fine thing," said Grampa. "An old man leaves the land of his birth to wander to God knows where."

"Not to God knows where," said Sidney's mom. "To the land of gold!"

Waiting on the platform of a small railroad station, Sidney saw a pair of brilliant, yellow, very long shoes with pointed toes. The man standing in them wore a bright green jacket and lavender vest.

"Mom! Mom!" whispered Sidney. "Look at his shoes!"

"Sh!"

"He doesn't understand Russian," Sidney assured her.

"Oh? He doesn't?" said the man in Russian, smiling.

Paris was Paris, there was nothing like Paris. In addition to the city, there was little Sidney's horse, bought in a Paris department store. He had never had a horse like this, so he named it Paris. Paris was black, with green eyes, stirrups, patent-leather reins, a leather saddle.

"Giddyap, Paris!"

One evening in Paris, discovering that one of the black reins was torn, Sidney threw himself on the floor, shouting, "My rein is torn! My rein is torn!"

"Stop that!" said his dad sternly, lifting him.

Sidney whimpered.

"Who could have done it?" his dad said, examining the rein.

"The maid?" suggested Sidney's mom.

"Grampa did it!" cried Sidney.

"How can you say such a thing?" his mom asked, looking shocked.

Grampa, stroking his long tea-colored beard, calmly observed the three of them from the sofa. His gray eyes looked mischievous.

"He did it! He did it!" Sidney shouted.

"Enough!" said his dad angrily.

Poor Paris, once so glorious. Oh Paris! Sidney started to cry—for his lost courtyard, for the little girl in blue, for the poppy fields, for the purple irises, and even for the land of gold to which he was going.

The Littles were back in Kiev to see Babi Yar. They had temporarily left the tour group, which they planned to rejoin in Leningrad, and were staying in the hotel they had used earlier. When they reached Babi Yar by cab they were disappointed to find that Babi Yar was no longer in the countryside. There were large apartment buildings nearby, and trolley cars, and fast traffic, and smog.

The artificial ravine, a shallow depression green with lawn grass, was almost entirely surrounded by groves of oak and maple. The monument, which they approached through a kind of park, consisted of a huge concrete base rising toward the sky and ending abruptly, as in a cliff. It supported dark, tormented, writhing human figures, some half-clothed, some naked, some suggesting they were falling into a pit. But powerful though the image was, it was very hard, it was almost impossible, for the Littles to mourn here, for the trolleys, the speeding cabs, the car traffic and the large apartment buildings were too forcefully in the present. Disappointed and frustrated a second time regarding Babi Yar, the Littles returned to their hotel.

"I'm bone tired," said Doris, stretching out on one of the twin beds.

"I'm going for a walk," Sid said, feeling irritable for some reason, and needing to be alone for a while.

"Remember to stay away from buildings. Walk close to the curb. Remember, we're alone here."

"Right."

Retracing the route he had taken earlier, he walked to the Central Market, pausing at the flower stand where Brigid, the Blue Girl, had surprised him by giving him purple irises, then proceeding to the broad boulevard again, with its strolling pedestrians under the massive, flowering chestnut trees. What a lovely boulevard this was. He would photograph the fountain, with its several geysers. He had meant to photograph it earlier but had been distracted.

"Hello, Dad! Surprise!" a woman behind him said. It was San Francisco Brigid, still in blue.

"Brigid!" he cried. Why was she still in Kiev? Was she visiting someone? An American? Maybe somebody in the consulate?

"I'm going up the street to the main post office," she said.

"May I join you?"

"Absolutely."

They strolled and chatted together. But soon, on an impulse, he said, "I'd like to take some pictures of the fountain. Why don't you go ahead. I'll meet you there," so they parted.

He took several shots. And then, as he was walking toward the post office, he heard a sound like thunder and saw clouds of smoke rising on the other side of the boulevard. People there were running, and screaming, and shouting hoarsely. Hurrying to see what had happened, he realized the smoke was concrete dust. He looked up. A large concrete balcony rail, as well as part of the concrete balcony itself, at the top of the eight-story post-office building had collapsed onto the rush-hour crowd. The top of the structure was now a maw.

He ran across the street. Human bodies were scattered on the sidewalk, some motionless, some writhing in pain. Blood everywhere. He thought of AIDS. Among the bodies was a red-headed figure in blue, lying on its back. Some of its clothes had been ripped off. Staring at white, soft, female breasts, he wondered at their whiteness.

"*Please* don't die! *Please* don't die!" he prayed silently.

And then he realized it was Brigid, the Blue Girl, and that her blond hair was bloody, and that, judging by the horrible condition of her head and face, she had to be mercifully dead. He broke into heavy sobbing, and remembered his daughter, Harriet, as a child, when she and he had had their little private "dates." And he was aware that a nearby middle-aged man was undergoing an important change. The right side of the man's face was frozen, and his chin was frozen to his left shoulder, and he was jabbering, "Waa waa waa waa waa waa waa!"

"He has something to *say*. And he's trying his best to *say* it," thought Sid.

Somehow, he managed to return to the hotel by cab and, again sobbing, told Doris what had happened.

"My God!" she cried, frowning fiercely while embracing him. "It could have been *you!* I can't *wait* to leave this God-forsaken country!"

Though she was upset, she nevertheless said she was famished and needed a snack right away, before dinner. He was unable to eat, so she went down to the dining room alone. Lying on his back on one of the beds, he stared at a ceiling pattern suggesting a horrified human face. It was terrible, Brigid's being killed on a foreign street. Her death felt acutely personal to him. She had called him Dad; had given him purple irises; had brought to mind Harriet, his daughter, who at times, currently, was as nutty as Doris had once been. He recalled the mysterious little girl of his childhood, dressed all in blue, and the night shelling of Akkerman, and the astounding sight of terrified adults, crouching in cellars. What irony. Thousands had been slaughtered at Babi Yar. Dick Gallagher was dying. Brigid was dead. Yet he, Little Sid Little, was alive and well. How to cope with his survival? It embarrassed him, made him anxious.

He should have stood by Brigid. But what could he have told the police? He didn't know the language. And the street had been filled with hysteria that had threatened to engulf him. He had come to this country in search of his lost past, and had found a bloody present. Feeling guilty, he tried for almost an hour to phone the American consulate in Kiev. The line was always busy, so he called the American embassy in Moscow and informed a baritone of what had happened to the young woman from San Francisco, blond, dressed in blue, whom he had known only as Brigid.

The following week he visited the Dick Gallaghers alone because Doris was shook up by the fresh news that daughter Harriet, married, with two children, a boy and a girl, had fallen in love with an older woman, her rich boss, and had already taken steps to get divorced.

"Richard isn't eating much now," said blond Nora Gallagher on greeting Sid at the door of her apartment on Confederate Street in the Village.

Sid remembered another blond—Brigid, with her straight hair. He *saw* her: energetic, husky, forthright; and saw her lying motionless on the Kiev sidewalk red with blood, an American killed by fraudulent concrete made by a fraudulent, man-eating political system. And he saw the Soviet victims lying with her, some writhing, some deathly still.

"He's afraid he'll throw up," Nora said. "He's been receiving a stream of visitors."

"Where does he find the strength, in his condition, to be so sociable?" Sid wondered. "Is he holding court? Is this his last chance to be royal in this life?"

Though the Nordic strain, strong in Nora, still contrasted with Dick's dark-Irish one, it seemed to Sid that it did so less effectively than before. She was aging almost by the week, especially in her face and throat, the skin of which looked looser and more wrinkled than he remembered. He felt a surge of empathy and sorrow for her that surprised him. He had been used to reacting to her in terms of her blond, foreign coolness, her uneven, somehow distant smile, and her aggressive ability to play the mother with him by thrusting moist food between his lips, and almost demanding an equally distasteful obit from him. But now she was Dick Gallagher's soon-to-be widow, caught between the demands of taking care of his dying and of no doubt frightening glimpses of her future.

"Richard is such a worrier about little things," she said, glancing at Sid as if asking for his help. "Now he's worried that the house may be infested with termites."

"So this is how it ends," thought Sid. "No sudden, blinding, exalting last vision. No spiritual breakthrough after a straight life. He's right to be worried about termites. They're munching away at his insides."

As they reached the second floor, Nora Gallagher said in her formal voice, which suggested traces of a regal manner, "This is Bill. Bill's going to shave Richard and trim his beard," and introduced him to an athletic-looking young man holding an electric razor. All three entered the master bedroom.

Hunched over, Dick Gallagher was sitting on the side of the bed, eyes closed, a white sheet draped tightly around him. His increased gauntness and extreme pallor startled and frightened Sid. But his naked feet looked solid, healthy, reassuring. Nora set some newspapers under them.

"So here's Dick Gallagher, on his way out, Lincoln beard and all," thought Sid Little. "Hi, Dick," he said, trying not to sound hearty, and trying to forget he had just returned from a major trip, whereas Dick Gallagher wasn't going anywhere any more. Opening his eyes briefly to glance at Sid, Dick Gallagher said nothing.

"It would be best to shave you at the vanity table," decided Bill, so Nora moved the newspapers while Bill fussed with the socket. Sid helped Dick cross the floor to the chair. As Dick sat down limply, eyes closed, his tall, lanky body tottered and almost fell. Nora stroked Dick's long, glossy hair from behind. Dick's gray stubble on the part of his face free of the beard was about a quarter of an inch long.

"The razor may pull," warned Bill. "Is it pulling?" he asked as he shaved.

"No, it's fine," Dick whispered.

But Bill decided the electric razor wouldn't do, so Nora and Sid helped Dick back to bed. As Sid put his arm around Dick, he thought, "He feels all bones. And resembles a concentration camp victim."

Nora and Bill left the room.

"How are you?" asked Sid, sitting down on a straight-back chair.

"Pretty good. Just weak," whispered Dick.

"How's your appetite?"

"I can barely eat solids now."

"Are you in pain?"

Silence. "Some," Dick finally replied.

Dick was lying on his right side, facing Sid. A thin brown blanket covered him. Mostly his eyes were shut as he spoke. Occasionally a dark eye opened. His cheeks and the whites of his eyes were now yellow with jaundice. Sid thought Dick's head had begun to resemble a skull. On the wall beyond the white bed, near a window sprinkled with sunlight, was a faded print of the Dali painting showing a melting watch.

"I feel bloated, strange," said Dick very slowly and with long pauses. "I had a CAT scan yesterday. When the radiologist read the result he looked shocked, then recovered himself and tried to look professional. He said my liver is free of cancer. But my bile duct is blocked. I could possibly have another operation to open my duct or bypass it. But the result would be extremely painful. And maybe I'd get one more week. I decided it's not worth it. The quality of my life wouldn't justify it. I've decided not to have any more medical help except sedatives and pain killers. This is such an unpleasant subject. I'm very sorry."

"Dick, I think you made the right decision. I love you," said Sid, trying not to sound emotional.

"It's reciprocated," Dick said in a very weak voice. "You've changed," he added after a pause.

"So have you," thought Sid Little. "How?" Sid asked.

"You look older. I'm going to be cremated."

"Nora told me you didn't want to be."

"I don't want to leave anything of myself behind. Except gold. I said to her yesterday, 'Be sure to have the gold yanked out of my mouth before I'm cremated. I don't want the undertaker to have it.'"

Sid laughed. "You're a card, Dick."

"I pay my respects increasingly to God now. I've been a terrible sinner, Sid. And I used to think I knew a lot. Now I know almost nothing."

"That's called wisdom."

"Or loss of memory," said Dick wryly.

There was a long silence, broken when Nora, entering, said, "Sid, I need to give Richard a shot now. But first I'll see you out."

"Morphine?" wondered Sid. "Life has changed here. I feel like a stranger."

Dick reached out a cold, bony hand, shook hands and, eyes avoiding Sid's, whispered, "Take care of yourself, old buddy."

Sid understood that this was their last good-bye.

"Good-bye, Dick," he said, and bent over and kissed Dick's gaunt cheek, the Lincoln beard of which was as healthy-looking as ever.

"*Now* will you write the obit?" asked Nora, the blond, sorrowful, distraught, vulnerable Scandinavian, looking intensely into Sid's eyes as she held the apartment door open for him.

"Yes," replied Sid readily, surprising himself. "Nora, if there's anything I can do—"

"Please stay in touch. Please always stay in touch, Sid. You *will* stay in touch?"

"Of course, Nora," said Sid, offering his warm, small, delicate hand as his eyes filled with tears.

She embraced him, squeezed him hard, suddenly kissed him on the mouth, and disappeared behind the closing door.